THE CATTLE DRIVE

When Jake Swindin agreed to deliver cattle to the Starr ranch in Wyoming, he was prepared for the difficulties. What he was not prepared for was waylaying rustlers. However, old Jake was a seasoned drover so he met the rustlers. That was when the real trouble started and there began an extraordinary alliance between John Doyle's professional rustlers and Jake Swindin and his riders . . .

JACK BONNER

THE CATTLE DRIVE

Complete and Unabridged

LINFORD
Leicester

First published in Great Britain in 1996 by
Robert Hale Limited
London

First Linford Edition
published 1997
by arrangement with
Robert Hale Limited
London

British Library CIP Data

Bonner, Jack
    The cattle drive.—Large print ed.—
Linford western library
    1. Western stories
    2. Large type books
    I. Title
    823.9'14 [F]

    ISBN 0–7089–5143–0

Published by
F. A. Thorpe (Publishing) Ltd.
Anstey, Leicestershire
Set by Words & Graphics Ltd.
Anstey, Leicestershire
Printed and bound in Great Britain by
T. J. International Ltd., Padstow, Cornwall

This book is printed on acid-free paper

1

Skunked!

H E sat his horse hidden from the open grassland by a fringe of pine trees. It helped too that there was no sun, just a high grey overcast.

He had heard them for close to an hour before they appeared, outriders, cattle; far back so as to be almost lost in the dust, two wagons, one with the high tailgate of a chuck wagon, the other a sturdy light rig loaded with blanket rolls, horse feed in sacks, extra harness, just in case, and the usual assortment of items hauled on long cattle drives.

He had difficulty counting the riders; sometimes it seemed like ten, other times he thought there were fifteen, but ten or fifteen, there were too many for his purpose.

1

He dismounted, rolled and lighted a smoke, squinted and told his horse it wasn't another drive of longhorn razor-backed critters that would fight a buzz saw, this time it was up-bred animals, with either white or brockle faces, heavier bodies and shorter legs.

Among the red-backs was an occasional brown Durham. In fact, he distinctly picked out two shorthorn bulls.

He knew more about the drive than people knew in areas where the drive had passed.

The drive was being made by a man named Swindin, a grizzled man who'd been making drives since his teens. He had hired out to make the drive for Alonzo Starr, one of the most successful cowmen in Wyoming's tumbleweed country.

After a while the watcher could hear cattle lowing. They were becoming irritable and wanted to stop, lowing, bawling and beginning to be testy about being driven.

He doused the smoke, got astride and turned easterly along the slope, never riding where he could be seen.

When he got back, John Doyle was lighting his pipe from a burning twig from their smokeless fire. Doyle was a large bony man with pale eyes, a bear-trap mouth, and fists the size of small hams.

He waited for the scout to care for his horse then went to meet him near the edge of their lush meadow which was completely cut off from the rest of the world by tier after tier of pines, and farther into the mountains, by fir trees, the variety which only grew at higher elevations.

John Doyle, a rugged, hard man, smiled as he addressed the younger man. "Was I right; it's Swindin?"

The lean, brown-eyed younger man nodded. "An' with a heap more than he usually drives."

Doyle watched the scout put hobbles on his horse as he spoke. "Is he headin' for the bony ridge crossing?"

The scout stood up nodding his head. "I couldn't get a decent count but it looked to me like he had somewhere around maybe a dozen men."

John Doyle pursed his lips in a soundless whistle, then smiled. "I'm surprised he'd try the same route again after what happened the last time. Maybe that's why he's got that many riders."

The scout nodded and started past toward the breakfast fire and hot coffee. John Doyle stopped him. "This time we'll do it different. He's been raided twice on the far side of the pass. This time we'll let him get well up into the forest, then we'll hit him."

The scout considered the big-boned older man from dead-level brown eyes. "They'll scatter to hell an' back. Gettin' them bunched will take a lot of time. Tryin' to work cattle in a forest means if you're lucky you only lose half."

John Doyle's square jaw got its rock-set position. "Whatever we recover will be found money. That big a

4

drive . . . we'll come off real good whether we find 'em all or not."

They went to the smokeless fire where two other men were sitting on bedrolls sipping black java. The seated men looked up. Before the scout could speak John Doyle relayed what the scout had told him, and added the other part — the business of hitting the herd in the middle and scattering Swindin cattle to hell and back in the mountains.

A lantern jawed man who was tall and broomstick thin emptied the dregs from a tin cup and asked the scout how far off the drive was.

"Maybe a day's travel, an' they're thirsty." The scout faced John Doyle. "That's what I was goin' to suggest; let 'em line up an' down the creek an' hit 'em when they're tankin' up."

John Doyle lifted his hat, vigorously scratched, reset the hat and shook his head. He then walked out where the hobbled horses were cropping grass and the three men around the fire said nothing. One of them handed the scout a full cup of coffee. The scout hunkered to sip it. It was too hot. He placed the cup on the ground, tipped back his hat and considered the other two men for a long moment before saying what he thought.

"We'll be lucky to gather a hunnert head once they get spooked and disappear among the damned trees."

The lantern-jawed individual wiped the inside of his tin cup with a swatch of curing grass as he shook his head at the scout. "He done made us money every other time. Besides, if we show up at Emmet's place with a big herd, it'd draw attention. Besides that, Emmet don't have the kind of graze a big herd will need . . . I think we better do it John Doyle's way."

The second rangeman was staring into the dwindling little fire and did not say a thing. He was dark with fine features, hair and eyes the colour of dark oil. His name was Carter Alvarado. He seemed oblivious to his companions as he stared unblinkingly into the dying fire.

The rawboned man returned to the camp. He had made up his mind the best place to stampede the Swindin drive was where the pass went uphill for several hundred yards before cresting and beginning to go downhill.

The creek was on the uphill side. It came out of nowhere, conveniently paralleled the pass for a short distance, then went underground.

John Doyle stretched out full length, tipped his hat over his face, an unnecessary thing to do; no sunlight reached the ground for miles excepting little clearings called 'parks' like the one the cattle thieves were using, and went to sleep, something his companions considered a genuine virtue. Not many men could go to sleep with their saddle-seat for a pillow when they were going to raid a large herd of cattle accompanied by possibly four times as many drovers as John Doyle had. They had perfected their tactic, which was to stampede the cattle and hunt down and bunch as many head as they could, trail them out and sell them.

Carter Alvarado chewed jerky, sat cross-legged staring into the fire until the nearest man said, "Horses are better. Cattle stealin' makes lots of risks a man don't have with horses."

From beneath his hat John Doyle said, "Cattle sell easier'n horses. Not everyone needs horses but everyone eats meat."

The talk ended among the men hunched around their little rocked-in fire. They slept like babies and awakened at first light. John sat up, cleared his pipes, rubbed his eyes and let go a large exclamation.

"Son of a bitch! The horses is gone!"

That announcement did more to make the others come to life with the alacrity only a bucket of cold water dumped on them could have equalled.

They went out where the animals

had been grazing and found four sets of hobbles lying in the grass. They searched half-heartedly then returned to the camp, and this time insult had been added to injury. All their saddle guns were gone.

John Doyle stamped around swearing until Carter Alvarado said, "That's a boot that fits both feet, an' somethin' else we better figure. Old Swindin's got some powerful good trackers an' horse thieves with his drive . . . an' they know we're here, an' most likely *why* we're here."

The unattractive lantern-jawed man, Orville Bean, suggested to John Doyle that with their presence known, they had one of two choices, and he mentioned the one he liked first. "Get the hell away from here."

"How?" John Doyle asked.

"Sneak down there tonight an' get our horses back an' stampede their remuda."

The scout snorted and scowled at Bean. "They'll have guards out, Orville.

From now on they'll be second-guessin' everything we do." The speaker looked at John Doyle who was sitting on his saddle blanket looking thoughtful. "It's no good, John. Even before, when we figured they didn't know we were layin' for 'em, the odds was too big. We go down to one of them towns we passed through gettin' up here, set down an' wait for the next drive."

Alvarado was rolling a smoke one-handed and did not take his eyes off what he was doing when he put in his two bits worth. "I give forty dollars for that horse. Nobody steals him without me gettin' him back."

John Doyle sat watching the last embers wink out. His announcement was no surprise. He said, "We need saddle stock. Settin' us afoot is the same as catchin' a rat in a snap trap. They know where our camp is; now that we're afoot they can hunt us down."

The rawboned man stood up and scowled. "If I didn't know better I'd say it was In'ians. Sneakin' in close enough to take the carbines too."

Alvarado was killing a smoke when he said, "How do you know it wasn't In'ians?"

The scout quietly said, "For all we know they're watchin' us right now."

For a long period nothing more was said but eventually John Doyle sounded peremptory when he told them that even if they were watched they should start walking.

Orville Bean groaned. As nearly as he could estimate it, the last town they had passed through was maybe ten, twelve miles south, smack-dab in the middle of as good a livestock country as a man could find.

The scout did not dispute the issue. He retrieved everything he valued and with the others started walking.

They had been on the trail about two hours when loud, derisive laughter reached them and John Doyle said, "Just keep walkin'," which is what they did. Occasionally Carter Alvarado looked in the direction of Swindin's cow camp and John Doyle growled at him. Occasionally too, they stopped to rest. At those resting places there was very little conversation. Orville Bean never stopped looking for whoever might be following them. Whoever he was — *if* he was — none of the other rustlers appeared worried, and that heightened Bean's anxiety.

When they passed down along the gently curving foothills toward grassland, they saw cattle grazing in all directions, two wagons, and riders.

John Doyle sank down on a punky old deadfall, mopped his forehead and sounded aggrieved when he said, "There's a damned fortune down there."

Carter Alvarado who had been counting riders, leaned toward John Doyle and spoke very quietly. "They're three riders short." Alvarado jerked his head rearward without saying another word.

It rankled John Doyle to hell and

back that hard-nosed old Swindin had skunked him. Not only skunked him but worse, had set him afoot.

They remained on the timbered slope until dusk, with only jerky to chew on and no water. When John Doyle came out of his reverie and said it was time to head for the nearest town, he also told them when they could see Swindin's remuda, if it wasn't too heavily guarded they might see about stealing back their horses.

The lantern-jawed man and the scout exchanged a sulphurous look. The remuda would be guarded, heavily guarded.

When they struck out farther back up the timbered slope several brilliant flashes which would be visible for a mile, caught what little light remained and sent a signal which none of the rustlers saw.

By the time they were parallel with the herd they smelled cooking food near the chuck wagon. Someone was playing on a mouth organ, not well but loudly enough for the skulkers west of the camp to hear every move.

The scout went ahead, was gone roughly half an hour and when he returned he had found the Swindin remuda, and guessed there were no less than twenty horses in it.

Orville said, "We only need four."

John Doyle asked about riders and the scout said there were twice as many men riding herd to keep the horses from quitting the bunch, and Carter Alvarado said, "In'ians do it all the time." He looked at Orville. "Want to try?"

John Doyle growled. "If anythin' upsets their remuda they'll sure as hell figure it's us."

Alvarado shrugged. "They know every step we been takin' up to now. I'm willin' to try cuttin' out a few horses, but if I'm lucky it'll be like kickin' a hornets' nest. There'll be riders goin' in every direction — an' us afoot."

For the first time John Doyle seemed

less than sure. He engaged Carter Alvarado in a long discussion about stealing horses, until Alvarado stood up, hitched his belt and said, "The best me'n Orville can do is cut out a few head. The worst we can do is stampede 'em an' set those bastards afoot like they done us."

John Doyle nodded, Carter Alvarado and Orville Bean disappeared into the night. John Doyle sat on his thinned-down bedroll listening and the scout, Davy Twigs, studied the high sky for a long time before lowering his head and showing a humourless little crooked smile at John Doyle as he said, "I think this will be my last raid."

The big-boned man misunderstood. "Hell, you can't expect to come up rich every time."

"It ain't that, John. It's never gettin' three decent meals in a row and doin' what we're doin' now, stumblin' around in the dark with cold comin', not to mention what'll happen if when daylight comes an' they see us."

Somewhere easterly a man shouted. The sound startled both the men who had been sitting westerly a fair distance talking.

The shout was followed by a gunshot, a brief silence then several gunshots.

The pair of rustlers were on their feet scarcely breathing and what could be expected to occur, did. Gunshots had startled the cattle out of their beds and sent them running in all directions.

John Doyle and his companion ran for their lives. Stampeding cattle only stay bunched if they can't spread out. Where John Doyle and Davy Twigs ran and kept running, wild-eyed cattle passed without even noticing them.

With cattle spreading in all directions the danger was being struck accidentally by night-blind cattle running in panic.

They found a tight little spit of young trees and got in among them. Cattle streamed past on both sides, some with lolling tongues and rib cages pumping.

John Doyle yelled to his companion

that if Orville and Carter Alvarado had started the stampede they had probably been trampled to mincemeat.

Without warning a rider flashed past the little grove of trees. Moments later two more ran past. The scout wagged his head. Not only were the riders too far behind to head off or turn the stampede, but they had blind-running horned cattle all around them. And what scout, Davy Twigs had anticipated, happened.

2

A Complication

THE Swindin rider quirted his horse hard enough to make it lurch ahead in leaps. A slab-sided brindle cow either heard or saw the rider coming and started to swing around. She didn't quite make it.

The noise of the collision was lost amid all the other sounds, but the men among the oaks heard it and saw the brindle cow go down while the rider and his mount fell across the cow who was frantically trying to rise.

The cow regained her footing and along with being frightened she was fighting mad. She pawed the inert rider, who appeared to the watchers to be either dead or unconscious.

The scout, Davy Twigs, didn't wait.

He left the oaks running. The cow was moving in the direction of the other cattle but not as handily, and the horse that had collided with her was standing with reins dangling within a yard or two of its rider, who did not move even after the scout caught his horse and the other rustler appeared.

The horse's lungs were pumping like a bellows. The scout took him in among the second-growth oaks and examined him. He did not appear to have been injured although it would have been a safe bet to say he was so badly shaken it wouldn't be wise to straddle him for a while.

John returned to the trees and told the scout the Swindin rider had broken his neck.

Davy Twigs's answer to that was they needed more horses.

John went to the south side of the little bosque to look and listen. There was plenty to be heard, shod horses running, panicked cattle bellowing, but there was nothing for John Doyle to see except an occasional winded cow standing head-hung with its mouth wide open.

Carter Alvarado and Orville Bean were missing. If they had been caught in the stampede they were dead. Davy offered to ride his acquired horse and make a search. John Doyle shook his head, there were Swindin riders in every direction.

Eventually the cattle and the Swindin riders got far enough south-westerly to make the lowing barely audible to the men among the white oaks.

Davy straddled his horse and told John Doyle he was going to make a little sashay, which Doyle did not approve of but Davy was already working his way among the trees.

John Doyle was sitting on an ancient deadfall tree when Orville Bean appeared. John nodded and said, "Whatever started it? Davy caught a horse. He's scoutin'."

If that announcement was supposed to cheer up the thin man, it didn't.

He was exhausted from charging cattle and night riding horsemen, but he said, "They done us a favour. There'll be cattle in the uplands. We don't have to bust into the middle of the drive to cause a stampede. Them gunshots done it for us . . . John?"

Doyle nodded and told the thin man to shut up, he was trying to guess where the horsemen were, something made difficult by roiled banners of dust. John Doyle waited with increasing anxiety for the scout and Carter Alvarado to return.

When they did eventually return they were leading saddled and bridled horses. No time was wasted, no questions were asked as John Doyle led them northward, back to the protection of the timbered uplands.

When he thought they were safe he set a precedent by hobbling his Swindin horse, dumping the gear in the grass and taking the horse to water.

What had happened provided grounds for doubt among the rustlers. As they were sitting in the verge of forest giants, Orville Bean said whoever was ramrodding the Swindin drive must have somehow anticipated an attack.

John Doyle wouldn't go that far although he intimated that never before had he been so abruptly routed, and that brought a comment from Carter Alvarado who was propped up by an upended saddle whittling off a corner of chewing tobacco when he said, "Nothing's gone right since we come up here. Maybe we'd better let this drive pass an' hunt us another one with fewer riders, in a place where no one's raided before." He got the cud tucked away and looked straight at John Doyle. "It wasn't no accident that there was so many of 'em, or that they somehow knew we was waitin'."

Neither Davy nor Orville commented, nor did they look in John Doyle's direction. As livestock thieves the four of them had worked together for some time and while there had never been a discussion about leadership it had somehow evolved that the large man was their leader.

What troubled them now was that they had been routed, which was better than being caught — which meant hanging — but they'd spent time preparing for this particular raid, and nothing had gone the way it was supposed to. When John Doyle tried placating them, giving reasons why things had worked against them it was his final statement they would remember.

"I got no idea where a drive that big can be found. All they know is that the cattle got stampeded. They don't know who or what stampeded 'em." John Doyle paused. None of the others were looking at him until he spoke again.

"Likely we can't get Swindin cattle, an' for a fact it'll take most of the ridin' season to find another drive — so — I got another idea. You remember that town called Mirage?"

They remembered and nodded.

"You remember seein' that brick buildin' in the centre of town? Well, it could take us a month or more to locate another drive so — "

Orville Bean interrupted. "Raid a bank, John?"

Doyle nodded. "Less plannin', less work, an' less danger. We can go back there, scout up the place an' take it from there."

The silence was so deep a distant magpie scolding something on the ground sounded clarion-clear.

Davy Twigs finally spoke. "It's right in the middle of the town, John, an' sure as hell's hot they got a lawman. Speakin' for myself, I like stealin' livestock better. A man's got more room to manoeuvre in. Town is like bein' caged to me."

John Doyle nodded understanding. He had once avoided such a raid as he was proposing, and had been the only survivor.

He had been seventeen at the time and had never forgotten the other two on the platform, ropes around their necks, nor the sickening sound when they had been dropped through the trap door.

Carter was still leaning against a saddle when he said, "How exactly do you go about robbin' a bank, John?"

"Not much different from rustling," Doyle replied. "You scout up the place, figure the best time, figure how you run for it afterwards."

Alvarado shook his head. "You ever robbed a bank?"

John Doyle barely nodded his head. Just that one time and for years afterwards he dreamt of the dead faces below the scaffold.

Alvarado had another question. "How do you find out if they got money?"

John replied using a tone of voice an adult would use to a child. "Banks always got money, Carter. Sometimes more'n other times. Money is their business, they always got it."

Alvarado said no more, but Davy Twigs and the skinny man did,

Orville wanted to know the procedure. "Simple," John Doyle explained. "One man at the tie-rack out front, another man just inside to keep watch from the front window, and two fellers to fill the sacks with money."

Carter dug out his clasp knife and went to work on a deadfall little limb nearby.

He listened to the others, for whom John Doyle was painting a word picture of irresistible promise and reward.

Alvarado went out where the Swindin horses were grazing — and froze beside a huge old fir tree. It was a long wait but eventually he saw it again — two men with Winchesters creeping around the southward tilt in the direction of the secluded place John Doyle had selected as their resting place.

He sidled from tree to tree, making good enough time. John, Orville and Davy Twigs were talking in a closed huddle.

He had to cross the clearing. He struck out, hands in pockets moving indifferently, endeavouring mightily to give the impression of a man with no pressing worries, and he made an excellent job of it. When he reached the huddle the skinny man said, "You should've heard, John's got it worked out."

Alvarado squatted like the others were doing and did not raise his voice when he said, "They're comin' around the south side, two I saw for a fact an' more'n likely others."

At the shocked looks he got Alvarado said he didn't think it would work, but they should go out and bring in the horses one at a time. He also said in his opinion they didn't stand the chance of a belch in a whirlwind.

John Doyle, Orville and Davy sat like stone looking straight at Alvarado, who arose, said he would go get a horse, and walked away. Their eyes were riveted on him.

The horse Alvarado had ridden had a large letter S on its left shoulder. It bobbed its head a little as the man approached but he chummed his way up close enough to slip his trouser belt around the animal's neck and turn back. He was acting his part perfectly.

The thin rustler put a hand on the ground at his side to push himself upright when John Doyle said, "Wait!" Orville relaxed but threw an annoyed look in the direction of the large man.

It wouldn't have made any difference if he had arisen.

Carter returned as unconcernedly as he had gone, and stopped where horse equipment had been dumped.

From behind them in the opposite direction from which they had been watching, a thin edged voice spoke clearly. "Steady as you go, lads . . . toss the guns away." They didn't have to act startled. They tossed their six-guns overhand behind where they were sitting, except for Carter; he tossed his pistol ahead. It landed between Carter and his companions. A different voice, deeper and tougher this time, said,

"You son of a bitch, leave the horse, pick up that gun and toss it toward the sound of my voice."

As Carter moved to obey he met the stares of his friends, picked up the gun and heaved it toward a stand of big trees.

The less menacing voice spoke again. "Now then, pull up your britches." When that was done and no hide-out weapon was visible, the thin voiced man said, "Stand up!"

They stood.

"Face around!"

They obeyed that order too, and a gruff, profane man exclaimed loudly: "That's them. That big one with the hair goin' every which way — that's John Doyle. He's the one I told you's got a bounty on his head!"

When they began moving into the clearing John Doyle breathed two words to Carter Alvarado. "US marshals!"

Carter studied the oncoming men, picking their way with saddleguns pointed, cocked and ready. One of them Carter was sure he had seen before, but try as he did, right at the moment he could not remember.

It looked like a church congregation. They kept advancing from among the big trees. A rough-looking older man, lined and weathered called to John Doyle, "I was right. I knew it'd be you. You done everythin' the way you raided me two years back. Doyle, along with bein' a cow stealin' son of a bitch, you ain't very smart." A sober-faced individual with a small circlet on his shirt front stopped about twenty feet from the rustlers, made a stingy small smile and addressed Alvarado. "I knew we'd cross paths again, Carter."

Alvarado, with hands shoulder high, palms forward, did not smile when he replied, "Can't say I'm glad to see you, Mister Hartley."

The formidable older man with a rangy, powerful build gave the next order.

"Set. An' keep your hands where I can see 'em."

As they sat the US marshal named Hartley approached Carter Alvarado, grounded his Winchester and leaned, showing that hint of a smile again. "From what Mr Swindin said I wondered if you wasn't one of 'em." Marshal Hartley removed the makings from a pocket and rolled a cigarette. After lighting it he tossed the sack in Alvarado's lap.

Alvarado made no move to lower his hands to roll a smoke and Marshal Hartley laughed.

Swindin went to squat in front of John Doyle and wag his head. "Twice in the same place? I figured you'd be in the country an' if you was that you'd try to raid me again, *but in almost the same place*? You must've robbed an asylum to recruit riders this time."

As the jack-booted burly man who in size and heft about equalled John Doyle, stood up looking triumphant, he said, "I lost a few head yestiddy, thanks to you, an' got a dead rider an' a couple got to ride in the grub wagon for a spell."

An unsmiling man came to take Jake Swindin over where two US marshals and several other men had been palavering. When he joined them one of the Swindin riders told his boss that the lawman wanted to take the prisoners to a federal prison and hold them there until they had been tried.

Swindin had about a dozen of his drovers with him. There were two US marshals and a couple of men they had brought with them from the town of Mirage because they didn't know the country.

Carter leaned to address John Doyle and a saddlegun barrel appeared out of nowhere and forced Alvarado to straighten up. He twisted for a rearward look. There wasn't just one gun-guard back there watching them, there were six.

The discussion among their captors only indifferently interested the rustlers. Carter Alvarado thought of John Doyle's scheme to rob a bank, and sighed.

To every man in the fullness of his years comes a reckoning. Alvarado had heard a priest say that when he'd been in his teens in south-western New Mexico Territory. For a fact, for Carter Alvarado it seemed that priest had been correct.

There was no alibi for their botched raid on Swindin's drive, particularly within a stone's throw of the Swindin horses and outfits.

Carter Alvarado and Davy Twigs managed to be close when one of the federal officers asked John Doyle if he knew some of his companions were outlaws. John Doyle's expression was blank as he shook his head. The other federal officer came up; he was much older than his partner in the law. He ignored Alvarado and Twigs, in fact had his back to them when he started to remonstrate with the younger federal lawman.

"Don't ask leadin' questions like that, for Chris'sake. They'll lie to you an' look you straight in the eye while

33

they're lyin'." The marshal paused, flicked a glance at Twigs and Alvarado and was about to continue his scolding when a gunshot sounded. It was so unexpected that for seconds no one moved nor made a sound. Then they bolted for cover, John Doyle and his companions too.

There really wasn't all that much cover. Most of the bushes did not have enough leaves to conceal a man.

Time passed. Whoever had fired did not do so again, nor did he speak. What made things particularly difficult was that the gunman had only fired one shot, it had been so unexpected that no one was sure from which direction it had come.

Marshal Hartley called loudly in his bull-bass voice. "Step out where we can see you!"

No one appeared. Hartley tried again. "I'm US Deputy Marshal Hartley. Me'n another federal officer is here arrestin' cattle thieves. You hear me? Show yourself!"

This time the silence was broken by the sound of a loping horse. The sound diminished as the unknown intruder got farther away.

John Doyle jerked his head for Carter, Orville and Davy Twigs to join him. As they moved in the direction of the loping horse neither of the federal lawmen made a move to either join them or order them to stop.

John Doyle was thoroughly bemused. Whoever the gunman was he had bought the rustlers time. What they eventually found was a shiny brass .44 cartridge casing.

As they were examining it the federal lawmen came up, appropriated the casing and scuffed for a yard or two for whatever else the shooter might have lost or deliberately left behind.

They found nothing and Jake Swindin took the initiative by telling everyone to get a-horseback. Only one or two men obeyed, the others stood like stones gazing at the cowman with obvious indecision.

When the marshals returned, herding Davy and Carter ahead, they put three men to guarding the rustlers and called a palaver among the others.

What bothered Marshal Hartley was, while of course they would have to head for Mirage, it would be a long ride, which could be interrupted any time that ghost-rider, or whoever he was, used his gun again.

A Swindin rider suggested that they ride skirmish style, a long line with a fair distance between each two riders, and in that way catch the invisible gunman.

A disgruntled man said, "An' suppose he's behind us? He can take us down one at a time. Naw; we got to ride together."

Marshal Hartley, presumably with experience in situations of this kind, told his younger companion to take two or three men and ride behind the main body. Whoever that gunman was, in order to create the confusion again that he had caused with his first shot, he would have to get close.

Carter told John Doyle it was a lousy idea but when they were being herded where the horses and horse equipment was scattered, John Doyle said nothing.

It required a fair amount of saddle-backing before they had the cow camp, with its wagons, in sight, and longer still to reach that spot, but when they did, and while everyone was busy caring for animals, Jake Swindin came out of 'possible' wagon bellowing like a bay steer.

His poke was gone. Every spare coin he had in the world had been in that cache. He was fit to be tied. "My workin' money," he exclaimed. "What I paid wages with!"

The federal officers went through the blanket rolls, extra lariat rope, all the sundries with which the wagon had been loaded. No one expected much and therefore was not disappointed when, after a minute search lasting almost two hours the federal officers came up with nothing.

Several quiet sour comments were made about this. Jake Swindin's exasperated disappointment was loudest. He said there was no way he could continue the drive without the wherewithal to pay for grain, watering rights, and the customary trespass fee ranchers charged for trespassers to cross their deeded land.

His loud lamentations, gestures and profanity pushed the dilemma of captured rustlers into the background.

How, he demanded of the Almighty with arms outstretched, was he to conclude his drive and get his payment?

The Almighty either did not hear or was otherwise occupied because he offered Jake no solution, but Carter Alvarado did. He said the cowman should drive his cattle down to that town called Mirage, and sell down until he had enough money to recover what he had lost.

If there was an alternative no one mentioned it, but Jake Swindin got red in the face when murmurs of approval came to his attention. He was a contract drover, the cattle did not belong to him.

He said, "No, by Gawd! I'll set right here until the varmint who stole my poke is caught. An' when he is I want just one chance to slit his pouch an' pull his leg through it."

3

The Unexpected

IT was as unlikely a roundup as was possible. Not only did two federal marshals participate but Swindin's hired riders rode with the men who had intended to steal as many Swindin cattle as they could.

Even with an augmented riding crew it required three days to make even a partial gather. Jake Swindin took John Doyle with him to help make a count, an open country drive-by, which never provided more than a guess-and-be-damned tally.

Both were experienced in making tallies but both came up with very different totals, and that exasperated Swindin who, around a supper fire accused John Doyle of deliberately coming up with a much lower figure than Swindin had reached, because, he said, John Doyle had done that in order to steal the missing number of cattle at the first opportunity.

Normally a statement like that was war-talk, but John Doyle did not miss a ladle of stew from the bowl to his mouth. In fact, an hour later when other topics had been discussed, John Doyle participated in the discussion as though Swindin had not as well as called him a conniving thief.

But later, with the fire down to embers and weary men shedding boots, shellbelts and hats before rolling into their soogans, John Doyle crossed the fire ring to tap Jake Swindin on the shoulder, and when Jake looked up, John Doyle jerked his head for Jake to follow him, which Jake did.

Not all the bedded-down men slept through it, but most did. In duration the scuffle was not long. Swindin was a strong man, but with age on him, as opposed to John Doyle who was also powerful, experienced in brawls and younger.

Swindin pawed to keep John Doyle away. When that did not work too well Swindin settled flat down and caught John Doyle coming in and stepped aside as Doyle went down, rolled over and slowly blinked several times before pushing himself upright.

Jake said, "This won't settle nothin'."

"You as well as called me a cow thief in front of the whole crew."

"You are a cow thief. We both know it. But right now that'll wait."

"Wait for what?"

"Gettin' the drive down close to Mirage."

"So's the lawmen can haul us in?"

Jake sighed, offered a large hand and used their grip to yank John Doyle to his feet. "Never mind the gawddamned lawmen. For helpin' make the drive, when we're close to the holdin' corrals down there, you'n your friends can disappear."

John Doyle looked hard at the drover.

"Are you havin' a change of heart, or what?"

"More'n likely a change of life. I've drove cattle for fifteen years an' I'm still ridin' the same saddle." Swindin gazed at the lumps of sleeping men and wagged his head. "When we get the drive to Mirage I'm goin' to telegraph the owner I quit, for him to send another crew to take the cattle the rest of the way."

John Doyle stared. He'd known Jake Swindin the drover for several years and what he did not know personally he'd heard from others. Jake Swindin never failed to deliver a drive.

Doyle loosened as he asked if Swindin was sick. The other man pulled a humourless small smile. "No, not sick, just a slow learner. In all the years I contracted to deliver drives I never done better'n break even. Somewhere along the trail I was bound to see the light. I expect tonight is the time. I wonder if there's any coffee left in that pot?"

Swindin led the way back. John Doyle followed quizzically eyeing the drover's back. He'd never heard a man say the things Swindin had said in all his born days. By the time they got to the fire, found a pair of tin cups and filled them with lukewarm java, John's bafflement was complete.

Around them men snored, not all, some were awake, watching and listening, but as Doyle and Swindin talked they did so in softer and quieter tones. Much that they said was indistinguishable. One of the listeners was the federal lawman named Arnold Hartley, and he gave up after a while, pulled down into his blankets and went back to sleep.

They were herding again the following morning before sunup. It was the opinion of those among them who knew the distance, that they would reach the plains around Mirage before sundown.

Hartley's companion, the deputy federal lawman named Stuart Showalter, was riding between Orville Bean and a

Swindin rider when he abruptly burst out laughing.

When a herdsman behind asked what was funny, the youthful federal marshal waved his hand. "Two federal lawmen, four rustlers and a drover's crew workin' together like we all peed through the same knot hole."

No one else laughed and when they let the cattle drift while they nooned beside a sump spring, Marshal Hartley took his companion to one side and while none of the others heard what passed between them, for the rest of the drive US Deputy Marshal Showalter did not even smile.

The grassland territory which surrounded the town of Mirage had been staked out and owned by cattlemen for some years. Jake Swindin explained this to Marshal Hartley. "They won't want no drive as big as this one lyin' over an' eatin' down their graze. When we come up this way we had to go far out an' around. Three landowners met us down south, give us a drawin' of what they said was forbidden land for free grazers, an' by now they've seen our dust. You understand what I'm sayin', Marshal?"

Hartley nodded. "I'll talk to 'em."

Before riding away Jake dryly said, "You do that, Marshal," and rode back to tell the others that he had warned Hartley, and the marshal had said he would take care of things.

Carter Alvarado watched sunlighted, dappled roofs of Mirage come closer. He told Davy Twigs he thought Marshal Hartley was nowhere as nearly as important as he thought he was.

The sun was close to its meridian when John Doyle, riding point with Orville Bean, sent word back that several horsemen and a top buggy were approaching.

With more than one stomach, cattle were not only everlastingly hungry but stopping a large herd in mid-drive was not at all like reining in a horse or using the binders to halt a wagon.

Jake Swindin wigwagged with his hat

for his riders to go back and forth to slow the drive, which they did as dust began rising.

What inevitably happened when a drive could not advance, happened now. Cattle began spreading out to the east and west. They lowed and bellowed, a continuous noise that never stopped. It was the natural reaction of animals who could not understand what was happening and expressed their bewilderment in the only way they knew.

The outriders accompanying the top buggy had to ride ahead to clear a path for the rig. Through dust it was possible to make out one of the pair of occupants of the buggy standing up, yelling and waving his hat.

John Doyle drew rein and halted. Carter Alvarado and Davy Twigs came up to sit nearby as they watched Jake Swindin and the pair of lawmen work their way through razorbacks to reach the buggy.

Doyle said, "Trouble," and continued

47

to sit and watch. Dust precluded detailed visibility but the man who had been standing in the rig waving his hat, alighted, hat in hand. His stance was bristling-stiff. the federal officers did not dismount.

From where herders could see the rig it was obvious that there was going to be trouble. The outriders closed in behind the federal lawmen.

John Doyle growled something and urged his horse in the direction of the buggy. Carter and Davy rode with him. The more ground they covered the more drovers joined them.

Orville Bean, who had been riding point, joined, the last drover to do so. The mounted men accompanying John Doyle numbered something like nine or ten horsemen. John Doyle set the pace, they couldn't have loped in any case; cattle were all around them.

The dust, the noise, the overhead sun bearing down, the anxiety and irritability of the cattle who needed water as well as graze, made the meeting around the buggy unlikely to produce anything concrete because when men talked they had to yell.

The arrival of John Doyle and his unsmiling companions caused a silence of those around the buggy. One man, holding his hat in one hand, large, red-faced, adamant and quarrelsome, still yelled above the noise, and hardly more than briefly scanned the new arrivals with John Doyle, except to include them in one of his big gestures as he bellowed that this land was deeded, it was not open range or free graze. It was owned by local stockmen who used it for winter feed and Jake Swindin's drive was eating feed the local stockmen needed for getting through the winter.

Marshal Hartley had gotten off his horse, he was facing the fiery-eyed man whose Prince Albert coat and matching britches indicated him to be a city man not a countryman.

His companion, sitting in the buggy, was still and silent. He watched the last contingent of riders come up and seemed to shrink inside his collar. He was smooth-faced, dressed as the angry man was, in a coat and trousers that matched, and a curly-brimmed derby hat that sat squarely atop his head.

John Doyle alighted, hitched his shellbelt and started toward the angry, red-faced, large man who gestured with his hat each time he spoke.

One of the outriders reined in to block Doyle's way. John stopped, looked up, met the outrider's menacing scowl with a look just as unfriendly, and slapped the outrider's horse on the rump. It tucked tail and would have jumped but its rider tightened the reins. The horse could only fidget.

Davy Twigs spoke to the outrider from close by. "Move your horse, mister."

The outrider sneered. Davy was not an impressive figure even on a horse. The outrider returned his attention to John Doyle. Davy spoke again. "*Now!*"

His six-gun barrel peeked above the saddle swells, and Davy cocked it.

The white-faced man in the buggy seemed to stop breathing. The outrider considered Davy, which was a mistake, while he and Davy were seeing who might blink first, John Doyle reached with both hands, caught hold of the outrider's shellbelt and shirt, and lifted the man from his saddle.

The haranguing, red-faced man stopped speaking. Every eye was fixed on John Doyle, who set the outrider on his feet, tossed the man's gun away and when the outrider started to hunch, John Doyle hit him alongside the jaw. The outrider went down and stayed down.

John Doyle pushed past until he was facing the large, red-faced man. When he stopped he didn't raise his voice. "You got somethin' to say, mister, say it in a few words, unless you're a preacher, then commence prayin'."

The red-faced man glared. "I'm sheriff of Bison County. Them cattle is trespassin' on deeded land. Unless they are drove off right damned now I got the authority to impound 'em under the law, an' sell 'em at public auction. You understand! An' who are you, anyway?"

"A drover. Helped bring these cattle down here."

"Then by Gawd you're as guilty as that other man."

"Guilty of what? Drivin' cattle?"

"Of trespassin', breakin' the law an' right now obstructin' justice."

John looked at Jake Swindin, who shrugged slightly without speaking.

John Doyle faced the angry sheriff. "All right, we'll move 'em off a ways."

"Every damned acre of this country is deeded. You know what that means? It's bought an' paid for land, an' the owners got legal deed to it. The only way you can drive them cattle is north. Up into the mountains an' beyond. Back the way you come."

John Doyle faced Jake Swindin. "It's up to you," he said, and the sheriff angrily brushed John Doyle's sleeve as he said, "It ain't up to nobody, mister! You trail them cattle north an' get 'em headed out right damned now!"

John Doyle eyed the sheriff. Before he could speak Marshal Hartley said, "How about if we corral 'em in the holding pens?"

The sheriff glared. "What good'd that do? You'd have to feed an' water 'em, an' in case you figure to railroad them out, there won't be no train down this line for ten days, an' even then it'll be haulin' passengers, not empty cattle cars." The sheriff was sweating, he'd had to shout to be heard above the sounds of restless cattle, and now when he stopped speaking he cleared his pipes.

John Doyle faced Jake Swindin to shrug as Swindin had done. The young federal marshal, who had said little, now spoke to the man in the buggy. "Until mornin' is all. They'll lose 'em in the mountains. It's gettin' along toward evenin', just until tomorrow morning."

The man in the rig had not spoken a word until now when he looked up at the youthful federal lawman. "It's not just the bank, Stuart. If that's all it was I'd stay until morning."

The sheriff turned on Marshal Showalter. "You heard! Now! Get 'em movin' now. Not in the mornin'."

The younger lawman again spoke to the man in the buggy. "It's in your lap, Charley, someone's goin' to get hurt directly. Overnight — hell — cattle sleep at night, they don't eat."

The man called Charley faced the angry sheriff. "That's right. They mostly sleep at night."

The sheriff snarled his reply. "You want to explain this to Mr Cogswell? He said when he left town — right damned now — no palaverin' just get the damned free-grazers off his winter feed!"

The white-faced man in the buggy looked up at the young marshal.

"That's what he said, Stuart. Get 'em off his winter feed right damned now."

John Doyle went over to speak quietly to Jake Swindin. Jake looked shocked, but stiffly he nodded his head.

John Doyle went among the riders, spoke quietly and when he had finished he walked back to the buggy and told the sheriff they would move the cattle. He got his horse, mounted it, nodded to the sheriff and led the riding crew, except for the pair of federal marshals, in the direction of the scattered cattle, where men split off to make a gather. The men by the buggy watched until the sheriff climbed in, unwound the lines and sat back to tell his companion, "That's the only way you can handle men like that." He leaned to ask the outrider John Doyle had knocked senseless if he could ride, got back an affirmative reply and settled back.

"They'll lose half them damned cattle in the mountains," he told his white-faced companion, and when the man beside him said nothing the sheriff twisted and said, "You know that young lawman?"

"He's my brother."

The sheriff's reaction was surprise. "The hell you say. He didn't want to foller you in the bankin' business?"

"No."

One of the outriders kneed up close and leaned to speak to the sheriff. "They ain't gatherin' 'em all."

The sheriff squinted out where riders were bringing in cattle. "If they leave any, I'll make up a posse, round 'em up an' impound 'em."

The outrider straightened up, did not move clear of the rig and watched the distant horsemen. He had worked cattle man and boy since he'd been a button. He was in his mid forties. He leaned down again to speak when one of the other outriders let go a string of profanity at about the same time the distant riders hurrahed the cattle into a wild run.

The sheriff sat like stone. What

he was watching was the deliberate stampeding of the cattle in all directions. His face reddened, he sawed the left line, turned the buggy and whipped the mare between the shafts into a run in the direction of town.

His outriders brought up the rear. One of them called to the other. "Now there's goin' to be hell to pay!"

The other outrider nodded without speaking.

From far out John Doyle and Jake Swindin watched. Swindin said, "We kicked the hornets' nest for a fact, John."

Doyle was reining around when he replied, "It'll be a while before we can make another gather."

Swindin derived less satisfaction from what they had done than did John Doyle. When dusk arrived and the riders converged, they headed up into the mountain clearing where the Swindin supply wagon would provide them with food. They did not reach that spot until full night was down.

While they were eating Jake asked if anyone remembered what that sheriff's name was. No one did, nor did it matter, their thoughts were about tomorrow, the next day and maybe a few days beyond.

Jake worried about the condition of the cattle, he was the only one who did.

Davy Twigs and a Swindin rider named Red Cartwright ate together; they had formed a friendship during the day, John Doyle noticed and shook his head. There were times in this life when things just plain got turned plumb around. Rustlers and drovers had been traditional enemies since the first cattle drive had been undertaken.

Cattle thieves by the score had been yanked over tree limbs; they just never expected, and never got, anything different.

When John Doyle went to his blankets he lay awake pondering the peculiarities of life among the living.

He did not give much thought about

tomorrow, but for a fact when rustlers threw in with legitimate drovers, and braced a loud-mouthed sheriff and the cowmen he represented, a very unusual condition had to exist. Losing sleep over the future was not worth it. John Doyle went to sleep, but Jake Swindin didn't. He had never bucked the law in his life. As he thought on it, that ringtailed sheriff would come tomorrow with a small army of deputized townsmen and, given enough time, with also a following of ranchers, and that, he told himself amounted to more trouble than a man deserved in several lifetimes. None of them missed the pair of federal officers.

Orville Bean had a breakfast fire going before the dew had begun to evaporate. When Carter Alvarado joined him wearing a poncho which had seen better days, they had to wait until the coffee was hot and by then everyone was grouped around the little fire, with nothing to say until they'd had their java, then they began acting more like human beings than hunched-up, wet-eyed, cooling-out corpses.

Carter spoke first about what was on every mind. "If we go down there an' commence roundin' up cattle, that subbitchin' sheriff an' as many idiots as he can dragoon, will be waitin'."

Skinny Orville Bean spoke in a lighter mood. "You know, I've been jailed four, five times, an' I can tell you a man can get used to bein' pampered: fed three times a day, a bed where wind an' rain can't get you. There's worse places to spend time."

No one was interested. They brought in the horses, cuffed them, saddled up and rode in a bunch down toward the open country. When they got there daylight was breaking and there were cattle grazing, the sun was brightening, smoke rose from the cooking fires down at Mirage, and Carter Alvarado said, "No sir!"

"No sir what?"

"No sir, they got to be down there waitin' for us. They're hidin' in arroyos, maybe they come up into the timber in the dark an' right now are behind us."

Davy Twigs said, "Well, you want to go back, you want to ride down there — what do you want to do?"

Swindin's riders looked at him. John Doyle's companions watched and waited.

John did not like it any better than had Carter Alvarado. As mad as that sheriff had been yesterday afternoon . . . "Tell you what," John Doyle said, "I got as good a runnin' horse as ever came down the line. I'll ride down there a-ways. If they rise up out of the ground I'll come back like I'm flyin' an' you boys cover my behind."

As he was reining away Davy Twigs said, "Them two federal marshals'll be among 'em. Watch for them."

John Doyle replied cryptically. "They're lawmen. Lawmen an' carrion eaters flock together."

4

Into the Uplands

THEY stood beside their animals watching. It began to seem that John Doyle was progressing farther than was wise. He rode around several bunches of cattle, paused once to look at the animals, and except for natural wariness the cattle did not run.

The rider who had cottoned to Davy Twigs, Red Cartwright, raised his right arm. Nothing was said, it did not have to be. A large party of mounted men were coming up-country from the direction of Mirage. The Swindin rider named Cartwright stood in his stirrups, placed two fingers in his mouth and emitted a high, piercing whistle. Whether John Doyle heard it or not he abruptly stopped, turned his horse and watched the distant horsemen then, without haste he lifted his mount over into a lope and headed for the waiting men below timberline.

When he joined the others Jake Swindin said, "They ain't ridin' to make a gather, they're headin' straight for us," Jake paused to expectorate before saying, "An' there's a hell of a lot of 'em." That last remark required no clarification. In the beautiful, clear morning even at a great distance it was not difficult to make a rough count. John Doyle said, "It's a small army."

Distances were difficult to gauge on dazzling clear mornings, but Davy thought there were about thirty riders, and Orville Bean added his two bits worth. "Comin' straight for us, like they know we're settin' here."

To that Jake Swindin said, "We're backgrounded by timber. My guess is that them two federal lawmen are guidin' 'em to our camp." And as though to emphasize that Jake turned his horse and the others followed him.

John Doyle got up beside Swindin, spoke briefly and when John Doyle changed course Jake went with him.

Red Cartwright the Swindin rider leaned to say he thought their leaders were going to leave tracks which would lead their pursuers away from the camp. Davy looked at the redheaded man riding stirrup with him. "You done this before?" he asked, and Cartwright wagged his head when he replied, "Ain't polite to ask personal questions."

Cartwright's guess was correct, they veered westerly from the trail that would have taken them to their camp, but as they worked their way past and around forest giants, Red Cartwright made another observation to Davy. "If them marshals is leadin' 'em, they won't follow us, they'll head straight for the camp." Red smiled wolfishly, "I'd say Mister Doyle's been a guerrilla; he's goin' to get up-country a piece, then cut easterly an' approach the camp with them boys in it, from above an' behind 'em."

Davy was willing to accept this theory, but being vastly outnumbered, it was his opinion that the Doyle and Swindin riders would be foolish to get into a fight. Maybe they could surprise the posse-riders from Mirage and the federal marshals, but when push came to shove there were not enough of them to make much of a stand.

Carter Alvarado worked past the others to reach the leaders. He told Jake sure as hell that big a posse would split off, half following the new tracks, half going straight for the camp.

John Doyle leaned to address Alvarado around Jake Swindin. "That's the idea. We can handle half."

Carter dubiously considered Doyle but said no more and when the closeness of big trees made it necessary, he dropped back.

Rarely did the sun penetrate past high treetops to reach the ground, but where that happened a light skiff of dust lingered after the riders passed.

It wasn't particularly arduous riding,

there were upthrusts to be avoided and ridden around, and there were high-country small meadows where horses could snatch something to eat as they passed along and, as always in high country, there were veins of cold-water creeks, shallow and narrow whose water chilled the teeth of men and animals.

Jake reined until Carter came abreast, then detailed him to drop back, watch for their pursuers, and return as quickly as he could to tell Swindin how far they were behind and how many had split off to follow the fresh tracks.

As Alvarado reined aside and the others passed, he waited until Orville came abreast, and told him to let the others pass. He wanted someone at the tail end of the fleeing riders he could contact in a hurry.

The sun was high, down-country in open grassland it was hot, in the uplands where sunlight rarely penetrated, it became as warm as it would be for the duration of the day. Warm and shadowy with layers of pine and fir needles underfoot which would take impressions and which would muffle sound.

Carter dismounted, listened and waited. He was alone with trouble coming toward him, not the most enviable position he had ever been in. He wanted to smoke but in a place where every scent carried considerable distances even though warm forest air seemed never to move, he postponed that urge.

When it seemed sufficient time had passed and no pursuers presaged their arrival with sounds, Carter led his horse deeper in among the trees and strained to hear. There was not a sound.

He worried; possibly the posse-riders had ignored fresh sign and had instead ridden directly to the camp.

He tethered the horse in a place of concealment, tugged loose the tie-down thong over his holstered belt-gun and began a slow and wary southward hike.

He heard a voice where he had

expected to hear horses. It was sharp-edged, words were indistinguishable but he knew that voice among shadows in the direction of his horse. They were either leading their animals or had left them and were scouting afoot, in either case they were following the fresh trail. Carter made a guess; there wouldn't be very many. He got back to his animal, untied it and continued to retreat parallel to the fresh trail, and nearly shot Orville who had come in from the east.

Where they met Carter motioned for silence. They waited in forest gloom.

This time it was a long wait but eventually a man spoke who seemed to be south and westerly. He did not raise his voice when he said, "There ain't no sign of 'em cuttin' back."

There was no acknowledging comment about that. Carter motioned for the skinny man to cross the trail and take a position behind a tree, his obvious plan was to surprise the possemen. Orville was not keen about this, they had no idea how many men they were going to ambush, but as sure as the Good Lord made sour apples it would be more than two.

Alvarado's mistake was made plain when, while they listened for the oncoming riders, and during a long moment of silence someone behind them cocked a gun. Orville twisted to look back. Carter dropped flat before also looking around. They saw no one, and for as long as they were seeking whoever had flanked them there was not a sound until a magpie made its raucous noise, and that brought both Alvarado and the thin man facing forward.

The magpie was answered by an owl. Carter holstered his weapon, glanced over where Orville was lying as though he'd turned to stone.

Whoever they were seemed to be in no hurry. The soft sound of heavy animals crushing needles had stopped.

Alvarado exchanged looks with the thin man then got up to sit with his back to a huge, rough-barked fir tree.

Bean remained belly down, seeking sound or movement in either direction. When it came it was a quiet voice to the east who said, "All right. Just get rid of the guns."

Orville obeyed without moving. Carter, sitting with his back to the fir tree was slower obeying but he eventually tossed his six-gun away. He also felt for his tobacco and was holding it in his right hand when the invisible man spoke.

"You against the tree — stand up."

Carter arose. It was not difficult to place the direction of the voice but finding its owner was something else.

Carter finally spoke. "All right, we're unarmed, what do you want?"

He got no response and leaned against his tree. Orville was as tense as a wound spring. Bad enough to be caught, but it was worse to be miles from anywhere with someone who might willingly commit murder.

When the next voice came it was from the south and close enough so that the speaker did not have to raise his voice. They both recognized the voice. The man said, "Left you boys behind, did they?"

Carter answered dryly. "Left us to guide you in, Sheriff."

That earned a blizzard of denunciatory profanity and finally a man appeared from behind a tree, six-gun cocked and levelled. "You bastard. I got a lass rope that'll make you forget bein' cute."

The sheriff was a thick man, dark and clearly bad-tempered. He told someone named Alf to get the weapons which were lying in pine needles. He then sent someone named Mort to use a pigging string to tie the hands behind the back of the 'damned thievin' outlaws'.

Four men stood clear of trees while two more went to do as the sheriff had ordered. While Carter was being tied he looked steadily at the sheriff. "What'd we do?"

The fierce-tempered lawman walked straight toward Alvarado, leathered his six-gun and struck Carter across the face. "You're goin' to learn some manners," he snarled. "You think this ain't serious? Where are the rest of your crew?"

Orville was holding his breath expecting Alvarado to give another testy answer. Instead Carter said, "Waitin' for you."

"Where?"

"Go on up the trail," Alvarado replied, and this time the sheriff called his part of the possemen to him and gave brusque orders.

"Stalk 'em like we been doin'. My guess is that they're as foolish as these two. No noise, spread out but like we been doin', go slow, they could be hid like these two was."

A coarse-featured man with bloodless lips and reddish hair said, "Shoot on sight?"

"No, damn it! I want as many alive as we can get. The scaffold down at Mirage'll handle four at a time."

The redheaded man was not satisfied. "Sheriff, I don't want to take a chance. If I see one I'll shoot him."

Instead of answering, the lawman detailed two men to lead the horses of their captives, and put a massive man with a cruel slash for a mouth who carried a big fleshing knife on his belt as well as cartridges in belt loops to take charge of the prisoners. His only order was, "Any noise, brain 'em."

They hadn't advanced more than perhaps twenty or thirty yards when the deathless silence was blown apart by a rattle of gunfire.

The sheriff held his left arm aloft, everyone halted. He gestured for a very dark man to scout easterly. Within moments the dark posseman was lost to sight.

While they waited the sheriff braced Carter Alvarado, for whom he had a particular dislike. "You know a man name Alonzo Starr?"

Carter could honestly reply, "No sir, I don't recollect ever hearin' the name. Why?"

The sheriff waited until the returning dark man had spoken to him before answering, and then all he said was, "You will, mister."

They resumed their stalk but now they angled more easterly, in the direction of the main trail.

Orville gave Alvarado an apprehensive look. Walking toward some kind of a fight, not only unarmed but with his hands tied in back was enough to make a man wish he'd listened to his mother, who, in Bean's case, had wanted him to become a Pentecostal preacher like his pa.

A horse whinnied, it was a short blast of sound which, like a single gunshot, came and went too quickly for its location to be detected.

The sheriff stopped them again. This time he sent the redheaded man to scout. His orders were short and specific. "They'll have watchers out. Don't do nothin'. Just find 'em. Bert, remember, don't start nothin'."

After the redheaded man departed the former scout, dark enough to be a 'breed of some kind spoke sullenly to the sheriff. "Why'd you send him, for Chris'sake?"

The sheriff replied softly, "Because he'll flush 'em."

The dark man's reply was unfavourably given. "Damned Irishman; he'll bust into 'em. He's got no control."

The sheriff nodded. "That's why I sent him."

The posseman regarded the sheriff stonily. He wanted the fiery-tempered Irishman to start a fight so the sheriff would know where the enemy was and how strong he was. He didn't give a damn if the redheaded man got killed.

It was a long wait. Too long for the impatient lawman. He jerked his head for the advance to be resumed. This time he told the large, cruel-looking man to shove their hostages out front, which was done.

Carter looked at the skinny man. Bean was moving like a sleepwalker. His ma had told him no one shoots preachers.

That horse nickered again. They were able to locate its position, not from the whinny but from the angry cursing and the sound of a hard blow landing which followed.

The sheriff made a sweep with his left arm and they changed course, bearing more westerly now, which interested Carter Alvarado because the camp was westward — unless, of course, Jake had decided to move westerly.

The sheriff stopped again, his forehead creased into a series of deep lines. The 'breed-looking man behind him said, "You see the sign, Mr Baron?"

The lawman did not reply. After a moment he moved ahead a few feet and stopped again. He picked up an old hat which blended perfectly with the fir needles, and again the sullen dark man spoke, "All right . . . now what?"

The bad-tempered lawman turned on the large 'breed. "You couldn't have done no better."

The 'breed did not back down. "I

could have done better with my eyes closed an' you know it." He swung his head from side to side. "Where are they? Ask Bert, Mr Baron."

The hulking 'breed had to know he had been pushing his luck. The sheriff was a fiery-tempered man. The 'breed neither lowered his eyes nor took a backward step.

Carter watched the lawman bunch for an attack, but none of them would ever know what might have happened, as a riderless horse with stirrups flapping came out of the gloom, wild-eyed and running. The possemen scattered. The horse ran through where they had been standing. One posseman made a lunge and missed, the horse disappeared among the trees.

Everyone was shaken. The sheriff peered ahead. One of his possemen said, "That warn't no horse that came up here with us. Likely it belongs to them cattle thieves."

This time when the sheriff faced the large, dark man he jerked his head. The 'breed walked away without a word and within moments was lost to sight.

Carter had been watching the dark, fiery-tempered lawman. After the incident of the loose horse the sheriff seemed less assured than he had before.

They all knew they were in an area of high risk and danger. What seemed to have shattered the sheriff's ability to lead and to command was the series of incidents which began with the disappearance of the redheaded man and concluded with the flight of a terrified horse no one recognized.

Alvarado was tempted to make suggestions. The reason he didn't was his knowledge of the unpredictability of the lawman's temperament.

When the large 'breed returned he had a six-gun shoved into the front of his britches. Without speaking he pulled the weapon out and offered it to the sheriff. Every man who had come into the uplands with the sheriff knew that gun. The redheaded man had been proud of it. A very talented individual somewhere down the years had made an inlay in silver of the Mexican eagle, snake in its mouth and all. There was probably no other six-gun like it.

The sheriff opened the side and spun the cylinder. While the cylinder was exposed he handed the gun to the 'breed, who nodded. He had already ascertained that every load had been shucked out of the gun. He closed the little loading chute, handed the gun back and said, "He wasn't no scout. I'd say from the looks of his hat someone come up behind him."

The sheriff was gazing at the gun in his hand. "Why unload the gun?" he asked.

The 'breed's reply was cryptic. "I got no answers, Mr Baron, but I can tell you one thing." He gestured toward the skinny hostage and Carter Alvarado. "Them two ain't the only ones likely to be snuck up on." The 'breed lowered his arm looking hard at the sheriff. "Mister Baron, if we keep goin' the way we been goin' we're not goin' to find our friends. I can smell a trap, for a damned fact."

Carter stared at the domineering, fierce-tempered lawman with a dawning suspicion. Sheriff Cliff Baron was not the first leader to abruptly succumb to things he could neither understand nor dominate.

He handed the Irishman's Colt back to the hulking 'breed, looked around, briefly met every gaze then addressed the 'breed. "We'll keep pressin' along until we run into somethin'."

The 'breed's gaze hardened. "You can, Mr Baron, but I ain't goin' to. I can tell you right now they ambushed Bert and sure as I'm standin' here they got us figured like we figured them hostages."

The sheriff's face reddened and when he spoke there was leashed fury in every word. "We're goin' on, and you're goin' with us," he told the 'breed. "Them others we split off from is up ahead somewhere."

He gestured, and for a moment it did not appear the hulking 'breed would obey, but he paused only long enough to reload the Irishman's sidearm from his shell belt then he started ahead, very carefully and very warily.

Men were sweating. The prisoners had no way to wipe sweat from their faces so they swung their heads. It helped but not for long.

Alvarado watched the big 'breed. If ever a man made an inviting target he was the man, and the way he went ahead, like a man walking on eggs, he certainly knew as much as Alvarado did about his peril. Once he halted to glance over his shoulder. The sheriff was behind him by no more than four or five yards. The 'breed continued ahead.

A way they could gauge his tension, was after only about thirty yards had been covered a screech owl screamed and the big 'breed leapt behind a huge tree so swiftly the others barely saw him move. Under different circumstances there would have been laughter. This time every man either dropped belly-down or did as the 'breed had done, got behind a tree.

The sheriff was behind a huge old over-ripe fir tree, the same forest mammoth the posseman called Alf had got behind.

When nothing happened after the owl screamed, Alf spoke in a half whisper to the sheriff. "You said in town this wasn't goin' to amount to much, there was only about six of them rustlers." Reproach was in every word. The sheriff glared at the younger man.

"That's all there is, maybe less'n six. What's the matter with you! When I called for posse-riders you was out front."

Alf did not speak again, he took down a deep breath, sprinted to the next large tree and pumping air like an old cow, did not look back at the tree he had shared with the sheriff. In fact his disillusionment, which had been increasing for some time, had crystallized into thorough dislike after what the sheriff had said to him when they had shared the same tree. The degrees of inherent courage varied from man to man, and wearing a gun had little to do with it.

5

Confusion

JAKE SWINDIN'S segment of the hunted riders had reached the camp and, knowing pursuers were somewhere behind them, had held a brief palaver. Mostly, the men wanted to leave the camp, but a few liked the idea of an ambush.

It was John Doyle the experienced outlaw with skill at avoiding the law who stated their position when he said, "Bushwhack? You damned fools, with half the men they'd ride right over the top of us. Get on your horses." As Doyle met Swindin's gaze he wagged his head in disgust.

They got astride and followed Doyle and his companion. Swindin watched Doyle. He had lived a fair length of time and had done many things, but never before had he even heard of drovers and cattle thieves teaming up together.

Jake got a fresh cud tucked into his cheek as he rode. However this damned mess ended, the man leading up ahead, the same man he'd have hung out of hand, was now his partner and that, by Gawd was something Jake Swindin could not have imagined in his wildest imaginings.

They hadn't gone far when a rider loomed out of the gloom with a cocked six-gun aimed. He shouted something which was lost in the sound of John Doyle's shot. The rider went off over the rump of his horse, writhed and tried to find his six-gun. His horse fled south-westerly. John Doyle drew rein beside the injured man, aimed his gun and sat there without saying a word.

The injured man had a bloody trouser-leg. He and Doyle exchanged a long look before the wounded man forgot the pistol and gripped his bloody leg with both hands.

John Doyle leathered his Colt, the others followed him and some distance ahead when they encountered one of those snow-water creeks and paused to tank up the horses, Davy Twigs asked how in the hell that posseman, or whoever he was, had gotten around and ahead of them.

John Doyle replied dourly. "We been wastin' time, that's how."

"The damned fool," Davy exclaimed and John Doyle agreed. "Every boot hill's got its share of damned fools. Likely, he was sent to scout, an' he sure-Lord did that. Quit talkin'."

They got astride and were surprised when the professional rustler began angling westerly. Jake rode up beside him to ask what he had in mind, and got a short reply. "Get over yonder where Alvarado an' them others are. Get over there up-country, so we can come down behind whoever else is over there."

The men following Doyle exchanged

looks but no one spoke again for a long while.

There was considerable daylight left, which was fortunate because John Doyle did not hasten. Somewhere, men had heard that gunshot and possibly the injured man's frightened horse had run through the area where those men were.

The next time they drew rein was after working their way through timber for some time, and this time John Doyle beckoned to Davy Twigs, and when they were close he said, "Scout ahead an' around. We got to be close to someone, either the fellers who went with Alvarado or the sheriff's crew. Be damned careful. My idea is to flank 'em, whoever they are. It'll ruin things if they see you."

Davy left the others riding slowly. Success or failure was riding with him and he knew it. Outnumbered, the Doyle-Swindin riders required a miracle, something Davy had never been convinced a person should expect.

While the others waited, standing

beside their horses, Jake leaned in solemn thought. Even if this mess came out well, even if that hot-tempered lawman didn't make trouble, there was the matter of the cattle, hundreds of them scattered, for all he knew, to hell and back by this time, and beyond that his promise of a delivery date for the cowman who had hired him to make the drive. Because it was customary, he and the wealthy cowman had hit upon a date with a 'more or less' clause, because, excluding the weather, it was a long drive. Professional drovers never allowed themselves to be pinned down to a specific date. Usually there was thirty days leeway one way or the other, mostly 'the other'.

Jake's projected date of arrival, plus the extra thirty days, would be up within another few weeks, and if a miracle happened right now, he and his riders would be unable to even gather the scattered critters, let alone complete the drive when the cowman expected them.

Jake was beside his horse pulling reins through his fingers, first one way then the other way when John Doyle came up and said, "You know, Mr Swindin, this trouble won't get settled one way or another for some time, an' right now I'd say, what with the numbers against us, we're likely to come out the wrong end of the horn."

Jake nodded without speaking.

The professional cattle thief had a little more to say. "I can't for the life of me figure out, exactly, how it come that I'm ridin' *with* you. It's against my religion."

Jake's eyes came up. "Religion?"

Before John Doyle could reply Davy Twigs came back leading his horse and clearly upset. Jake and John Doyle went to meet him.

"They're thicker than the hair on a dog's back. I think the ones that split off, that set about layin' a false trail is over there." Davy paused to suck air before continuing. "They're in a sort of half circle behind trees. Must be maybe fifteen of 'em."

Jake had a question. "Did you see them federal lawmen?"

Davy nodded. "There's somethin' goin' on. They ain't watchin' behind, they're lookin' southward."

John Doyle spat aside as Davy Twigs offered an idea he had hatched on his ride back. "I seen that redheaded feller who was with the sheriff. He was trussed like a turkey. He'd been hit, there was dryin' blood on him. My notion is, if we can get behind 'em, then sneak down close — "

"How many?" Jake Swindin asked.

Because he had already been asked that question the scout generalized. "I don't know. You want a guess? I'd say about fifteen, maybe more'n maybe less." As he stopped answering Jake, the scout turned his attention back to John Doyle who, in anticipation of Twig's restatement of his plan, spoke first. "How far ahead?"

"Half, three-quarters of a mile."

The rustler's next remark stopped Davy in mid-breath. "You stay here'n mind the horses. The rest of us'll go find their remuda."

Davy recovered from the shock of being left behind to say, "They got two men with saddleguns mindin' the horses, which is north of where the others are. If you kept goin' due west like we been doin', you'll come on to their animals."

John Doyle said it again, looking Davy straight in the eye. "You stay back an' mind the horses . . . Davy, if we can set 'em afoot they're goin' to come horse-huntin' like a nest of bees. You understand?"

Davy nodded, mollified because his chore as a horse-mincer had been lifted from the chore-boy category to something more exalted. His job would be to prevent the horses from being appropriated by a number of afoot possemen.

John Doyle led them afoot, each man walking gun in hand, and Jake

Swindin staying up front. It was not a very impressive party, too few men for the bold undertaking John Doyle had in mind. If they had doubts it would have helped dispel them if they had known more about John Doyle both before and after he became a rustler.

Somewhere ahead they heard men shouting back and forth. Jake threw up his arm, they all stopped to listen. Before Jake could speak Davy said, "Hell, that's Carter."

Jake cocked his head before saying. "The other one's that sheriff from Mirage."

Cartwright, who had said very little up until now, spoke quietly. "While they're palaverin' let's find them horses. Since Jake can't pay us now, we'll be headin' home."

John Doyle led off again with Jake Swindin slightly in advance. Dust rose, did not dissipate but hung in the air as they passed.

Jake halted and raised his arm, then dropped to one knee, the others followed Swindin's example with no idea what had prompted the drover's action.

Within moments they heard the sound Jake had detected. It was muted and except that more than one creature was making it, might not have been detected.

Jake said, "Horses," and John Doyle arose to stalk ahead. They followed him, and if there had ever been doubt about the cow thief's ability to stalk, it was dispelled now. Part of the time he disappeared then reappeared. Cartwright softly spoke to himself, "Better'n an In'ian, he is."

It eventually became possible to discern through the trees that peculiar forest dust which arose and did not fall back nor dissipate.

The smell was unmistakable. They had found the remuda. Possibly because at this crucial stage John Doyle preferred not to take chances, he gestured for the others to remain among the trees and again scouted ahead.

Success depended on the rustler. If he failed and aroused the possemen, even if they fought like tigers the end would be inevitable given the disparity in numbers.

They waited, sweated and strained for sounds. The horses were probably thirsty because they milled and profanity from the exasperated men detailed to watch did not help. Animals go by the sound of a man's voice not by the words and those *remuderos* were understandably clearly agitated.

As suddenly as the outlaw had faded he returned the same way, from the north. He sank to one knee using a stick for support.

Using a twig he swept needles to make a slight clearing and made a diagram as he spoke. "This is where the remuda is. Like Davy said, it's got two guards. They're havin' a time of it to keep the horses from gettin' clear. Thirsty, I'd guess. We'll go up-country. When we come down near the horses there's some big rocks. They'll shield us right up close enough."

John Doyle tossed the stick aside. "They got one of the sheriff's possemen. He's tied to a tree an' like Davy said, he's been hit an' is bloody."

"That hollerin' back an' forth is because the sheriff's got Alvarado an' Bean. He's offerin' them for the right of him an' his friends to ride back down out of here."

Jake frowned. "That don't make sense. The sheriff's *with* them possemen."

John Doyle smiled, something he rarely did. "I got a notion the part that split off to find Alvarado ain't partial to the sheriff. They're actin' like renegades. The way it looks to me, whatever their reason, they're buckin' both sides, us an' the sheriff."

Jake was not satisfied so he said, "John, they come up here with the sheriff."

Doyle looked at the drover, and for a moment was silent before he spoke. "It's anyone's guess why men do things. You know that as well as I do. Maybe they rode with the sheriff in case some of us got bounties out on us. Maybe somethin' else. All I can say right now is that sheriff's in trouble over yonder an' it's damned confusin'. Maybe Alvarado'll know what's goin' on." Doyle straightened. To Davy Twigs he said, "Be careful. If it looks like someone's scoutin' you up, move the horses . . . all right let's go."

If there was an advantage to several men trying to stampede the horse herd of a lot of men, it had to be that the men following John Doyle would make less noise, and were being led by a known cow thief who, it could reasonably be supposed, had stampeded stolen horses before.

None of this entered the mind of John Doyle's followers. Even Jake Swindin, who'd had occasional flashes of doubt and bafflement, followed John Doyle as warily and as quietly as he could.

When they were north-westerly far enough, they could hear men calling back and forth. Only once did a clear exchange reach them. That was when a man with a foghorn voice said, "Sheriff, you said there'd be reward money. All we had to do was find 'em, surround 'em an' take 'em. Well — there's been surroundin' goin' on an' so far you ain't kept your word about bounties."

The reply, also spoken loudly and angrily was fiercely stated. "You damned fools. You're turnin' renegade." The angry voice stopped, when the sheriff resumed speaking he was clearly exercising self-control at great effort. "You'll get your share of the bounty money. I happen to know that drover figured to meet some rustlers an' together they was fixin' to steal the whole drive."

Jake Swindin almost stumbled when he heard this. John Doyle caught him by the arm, put his finger to his lips and shook his head. It almost worked. Jake said, "That lyin' son of a bitch!"

John Doyle shook the cowman lightly, wagged his head and pressed forward through forest giants.

The exchange southward continued for a while. The way it ended was when the man with the foghorn voice said, "All right, Mr Baron, you can come ahead, guns leathered an' both hands in plain sight. But you don't lead the posse no more."

John Doyle picked up the pace a little as they moved southward like wraiths in forest gloom dodging huge trees without making a sound, but raising small wisps of ancient dust.

The rocks were in a small clearing where no trees could grow, but there were trees all around except southward, and the trees in that direction were spaced far apart. Whatever had caused this phenomenon had occurred aeons ago. Every forest had similar small mysteries. The closer one got to rimrocks, the more these unique places appeared.

John Doyle reached the first boulders, too small to hide a man if he stood erect, and worked his way deeper until the rocks were huge, massive enough to conceal a mounted man.

Here, with voices closer, he sashayed until he found openings. No one had to be told where to hide. As they got into position one of the horse tenders looked up-country as though he might have heard something. His companion, with a Winchester in the crock of one arm was concentrating on the noise southward.

Davy and John Doyle had been right, the horses were restless. Several stopped dead-still, little ears pointing in the direction of the rocks.

One of the chore-men spoke to his companion. "They'd ought to hang Cliff Baron. He got us into this mess. Him an' his worthless damned promises."

The other horse guard faced slowly forward. He was distinctly uneasy. Simple, straightforward men require straightforward situations, which this was certainly not. He and his companions had taken sides with the other disgruntled possemen. For a fact the sheriff was not liked even in town, but he was — or had been — a leader. Without him the posse-riders were unable to unanimously decide anything — except that all were sick and tired of the present mess. Bounties or not all they now wanted was to get the hell out of the up-country. That talk of bounty money was a restraint, but the longer this complicated damned mess continued, the less even the promise of reward money provided an inducement.

Their backs were to the men in the rocks, no more than ten or twenty yards northward, but both men had Winchesters.

John Doyle leaned on a rock looking southward, but not for long. When he pulled back he gestured for Jake to meet him. Where they came together John Doyle said, "Stay here. I'm goin' westerly an' come in from the trees. When I commence shootin' you do the same. I'd like the horses to stampede down through where them fellers are, scatter 'em too, but if they run westerly an' you shoot it'll set them to really runnin'."

Jake nodded. John Doyle got behind rocks as far as he could go, gauged the infrequent timber where he would be visible when he ran, set a course and ran.

The distance was not great, no more than four or five hundred feet before dense tiers of huge trees provided concealment, and right up until Doyle made his run the haranguing southward ensured that all attention was in that direction, but when John Doyle was midway someone squawked an alarm and pointed. For moments the seekers did not see the running man, but eventually they did because movement attracted and held attention anywhere. It was historically that where there was upright movement it was made by animals that ran on legs, two or four.

Jake heard the shouting. He also saw the first man to fire. It was the sheriff. John Doyle made the thick timber sucking air with a heartbeat that sounded loud enough to him to be heard some distance.

There were several more shots, this time from Winchesters. Jake chose this time to get down closer through the rocks. He could have picked off the pair of horse-guards with his eyes closed and the temptation was strong. He thought that since the possemen had seen someone running westerly, they would guess his reason and double the guards at the remuda. If Jake fired now, the gunfire would start the horses running.

He was snugging back his saddlegun when a rattle of shots came from the foremost rank of forest giants westerly. They were not random shots, in fact one bullet struck a huge rock near Jake, who flinched and got flat.

Pieces of ancient stone flew in all directions. Some hit the loose-stock. Other shots dropped green limbs among the animals. The last pair of shots ploughed earth less than twenty feet from the horse-tenders. They had been straining to find a target. After the pair of near-misses they fled. Seconds later the entire remuda pawed dust tree-top high as horses stampeded in all directions. Several went down through the area where the arguing possemen were, not only forcing some possemen to run for their lives, but also charged blindly southward down where the sheriff was.

The stampede was a success, roils of ancient-smelling tantawny dust rose. Men eventually called to one another. All Jake Swindin had to do was push his pistol barrel between two rocks. The fleeing horse-guards were racing toward protection of the rocks. All Jake had to do was confront them with his cocked six-gun, and when they halted told them to put both hands atop their heads. The horse-guards were breathing hard. They were also round-eyed. Jake walked down, disarmed them and shook his head as he growled, "Damned fools."

He brought his pair of prisoners back through the rocks, paused to study them and to listen to the turmoil southward.

He smiled and wagged his head. The possemen watched him with apprehensive expressions. They did not know who Jake Swindin was, what they *did* know was what the sheriff had told them down in Mirage while he was acquiring posse-riders.

The worst, most deadly dangerous renegade in the territory was the leader of the men the sheriff meant to run to earth and hang. There was no one fitting the description among the stockmen opposing the possemen, which they *did* not know, but they did know something else the sheriff had said was a damned lie. Catching the men he wanted would be as easy as falling off a log.

6

Six-Guns and Pandemonium

JOHN DOYLE was short of breath when he rejoined the men among the rocks. He exchanged long looks with the hostage horse-herders and while tumult reigned elsewhere, in the rock field where it was relatively quiet, Doyle asked the captives just what in the hell was happening among the possemen.

One captive, a whiskery-faced individual with sunk-set eyes which did not move from John Doyle's face explained in short sentences.

He started out with a question. "You know Sheriff Baron?" and when John Doyle shook his head the captive loosened a little. "He got up a posse in town sayin' there was rewards for you fellers, an' that one of you was a notorious outlaw. So we come with him. Thing is, mister, only outlaw we caught was a redheaded feller, friend of the sheriff. An' now with our ridin' stock gone . . . Most of us is disgusted. The sheriff said it would be easy to surround a few renegades and capture or kill 'em, and that was a damned lie. He got us into a gawdamned war."

Jake Swindin asked the beard-stubbled man if he thought Sheriff Baron would give up and go back, and the captive wagged his head as he switched his attention to the large man. "Maybe some will go back, but the sheriff'll have as many men as he can influence." The posseman had a question of his own. "Which of you gents has a five hunnert dollar bounty on you?"

Jake stared. John Doyle regarded the beard-stubbled rangeman dourly. "Is that what he told you?"

"Yep. Some of us talked it over and come to the conclusion it was a lie. Is it?"

John Doyle made a cold, hard smile. "You think with that kind of bounty, any of us'd be workin' cattle?"

"No," the captive replied. "An' that's what the others figured." He faced his companion, the second captive, who had not said a word thus far, and spoke quietly. "Jimmy . . . ?"

The man called Jimmy spat aside before speaking. "All I want is to get the hell back to town. I've rode my butt raw, missed meals, been shot at . . . all I want is to get the hell back down out of here."

John Doyle studied this captive before asking how he and his companions could get the sheriff. The posse-rider answered without hesitation. "Find the son of a bitch. When you do there won't be much trouble. He's still got a few fellers friendly to him, but not many. My guess is that they'll try to recover the horses, an' most likely they'll catch a few, but that ain't goin' to set well with the fellers who are still afoot."

Jake addressed John Doyle. "Spread out an' stalk."

John Doyle nodded while looking at the captives. "You boys come with me," he said, and cupped both hands around his mouth as he called loudly, "Alvarado. Carter Alvarado, you hear me?"

There was no answer. Before they split up John Doyle said their friends as well as their enemies were in the forest, for no one to shoot unless he had to. Something that did not need to be said but Doyle felt better for having said it.

There were sounds in three directions, south, east and northward.

Most of the horse-hunters seemed to be south-easterly, which was the way John Doyle went with his captives, using them out front to scout for him.

The captives, both taciturn individuals, did not appear to object to their new role. They had been among the foremost to denounce the sheriff. John Doyle did not ask the most reticent of the pair his name. Right at the moment it did not matter, but it was this nameless posseman, short and powerfully built who was some distance ahead of his friend and his captor, who suddenly dropped to the ground.

The others did the same. The nameless man twisted to address his companion in a husky whisper. "Watch ahead'n southward."

John Doyle took his advice. What he eventually saw, moving among big trees like wraiths, were two men. He recognized one man and cupped his hands to softly call, "Alvarado!"

The ghosts vanished in a twinkling.

John Doyle called again. "Alvarado! It's John Doyle north of you a piece."

There was no reply nor movement that the man lying belly down could distinguish. As time passed one of the captives twisted to address John Doyle. "You sure? Mister, the way them lads hid I got an idea they ain't your friends."

John Doyle raised up on his forearms like a lizard and scanned in all directions. He was still propped like that when a voice he recognized spoke quietly from among the big trees northerly.

"Mister Doyle, good to see you."

Alvarado came out of hiding, looked askance at the captives with empty holsters, stopped as John Doyle arose as Orville Bean, sweating like a stud horse, grinned at John Doyle. He had the expression of a frightened rabbit. His interest in the empty-holstered captives was less casual. In fact as John Doyle talked Orville stood back intently watching the captives, one of whom produced a plug, gnawed off a corner and offered the plug to Orville, who shook his head. The other captive also nibbled off a cud before returning the plug to its owner. This captive, the man with the sunk-set eyes, considered Orville with veiled amusement.

When the palaver was finished Carter and Orville went southward to join the sweep John Doyle was making. When they finally heard horses and came close, something behind them brought them briefly erect before each man hid among the trees.

Two armed possemen appeared, not taking any particular precaution as they weaved in and out of tall timber. Both had Winchesters as well as belt guns. Without warning Carter Alvarado spoke; the words were not loud but the two strangers stopped stone still. Carter spoke again.

"I thought you fellers said you was headin' down out of here."

One of the strangers faced the sound of Carter's voice as he replied, "Alvarado? What'n hell you doin' way over here?"

"Same as you, lookin' for horses."

Alvarado stepped into sight as he called softly to his friends. "It's Alf and Mort, posse-riders from Mirage. When I got caught they cut me loose."

Carter stopped in front of the posse-riders. "Could one of you gents loan me a gun?"

Both Alf and Mort eyed Alvarado

as though they'd been asked for an ounce of blood. John Doyle stepped in front of the skinny man, lifted away his six-gun and tossed it to Alvarado. To Orville he said, "You can have the other one's carbine."

A rider was approaching up-country. Since it was not possible to maintain absolute silence where a number of horses were concerned the southerly listeners stood like statues. Carter nodded at John Doyle. "I'll scout 'em up." Doyle offered no objection so Carter went swiftly and soundlessly northward. The others heard two voices, the sound of horses stopped, and Carter returned ahead of Davy Twigs leading the horses he had been left to guard. As he was dismounting, Twigs said, "It sounded like all hell busted loose. Next thing I knew men was callin' back an' forth as they run among the trees. I figured I'd better do what John Doyle said, keep clear of whoever was comin' toward me, so I rode my horse an' led the others." Davy paused to expel an unsteady breath. "What in the hell happened? I heard loose stock run in all directions."

No one offered much of an explanation, the men who owned the horses Davy had brought went to them, took the reins, checked cinches and mounted, which left the pair of posse-riders afoot. The man called Alf said, "Find a couple more horses. We'll tag along on foot."

Someone had caught horses. Swindin's companions could hear them calling back and forth as they headed southward. Jake told John Doyle some of the posse-riders were heading home and Doyle nodded. He told the two horse-guarding captives they could leave if they wanted to. They nodded and disappeared into the trees.

Sounds of horse-hunting possemen diminished the farther east they went. When Jake and John Doyle arrived on a timbered bluff overlooking an immense stretch of treeless grassland they saw neither mounted men or those on foot.

They had, Jake thought, out-distanced the horse-hunters. Whether John Doyle agreed or not, probably not, two men emerging from a log barn where there was a scattering of buildings up ahead, who looked not much larger than ants, kept him as well as the others still and silent.

One of these distant figures pulled a top buggy by the shafts from the barn. Moments later the other man led forth a driving horse.

John Doyle foraged for a trail downward from the barranca and by the time he had found one the two men left their yard driving in a south-westerly direction toward the distant town of Mirage.

It required more than half an hour to get down from the bluff and across the intervening distance to the clutch of ranch buildings. Alf and Mort were dog-tired by the time the small cavalcade roused up a pair of dogs as they crossed the yard toward the corrals and barn.

They tied up out front and went into the barn looking for saddle stock. They found several using horses in one of the corrals out back which Mort and Alf greeted with genuine warmth.

Inside, they borrowed two bridles, blankets and saddles. While the pair of possemen were rigging out John Doyle led the others out front — right into the faces of two grim-faced, resolute women holding double-barrelled scatterguns. Each woman had the dog on one barrel of their weapons hauled back at full cock.

For seconds not a word was said. John Doyle's expression was set in stone. Jake Swindin took down a big breath and seemed to be holding it.

Garter Alvarado smiled at the women and lied with a clear conscience. "Ladies, we need two horses to mount a couple of our friends who lost their animals in a fight back up yonder when some possemen, cowmen an' rustlers come together."

The oldest woman had grey-streaked hair pulled severely back in a bun. Everything about her stance and expression said she was a no-nonsense individual when she dryly said, "An' you'll be possemen."

Carter still smiled when he shook his head. "No, ma'am. We're stockmen."

The stone-faced woman spoke again. "We heard gunfire comin' from the timbered country westerly. My husband an' hired man went to Mirage to find the sheriff."

Alvarado had no difficulty answering this time. "They won't find him, ma'am. He's back up yonder. He come up there with posse-riders. They're scourin' the country."

The younger woman had a peaches-and-cream complexion, dark blue eyes and a long braid of light hair down her back. She shifted the shotgun as though unaccustomed to its weight and the watching men held their breath. Not all scatterguns had hair triggers, but some did.

116

The older woman looked from one man to another. She did this slowly and thoughtfully before she said, "Well, shed your weapons. We'll go over to the house an' set until my husband gets back."

Alvarado replied almost curtly. "Ladies, we got to keep ridin'. Them outlaws is around an' we got to find 'em. We been followin' their sign."

"They didn't come here, young man," the woman replied curtly. "But you did."

"They dassn't come to a ranch, ma'am." Alvarado switched his attention to the younger woman who had been watching him closely. His smile widened but before he could speak the older woman said, "Get rid of your guns!"

From the south side of the barn a man spoke harshly. "Ease down the dogs on them shotguns and put them on the ground." It appeared for a moment that the older woman was not going to obey.

The next masculine voice spoke from the north side of the barn. It was less menacing. "Put 'em down, ladies. Real easy."

The pretty young woman looked at her companion. The older woman eased the hammer down while looking daggers at Carter Alvarado, leaned swiftly and put her shotgun on the ground. The younger woman did the same.

Alf and Mort came from both sides of the barn and Alf shook his head at the older woman. "If you seen us come into the yard you knew how many we was. When you braced the fellers out front — if you can count — you should've known there was two unaccounted for."

Alf picked up the shotguns, tossed them into the barn, traded hard stares with the older woman then said, "All right, let's go to the house, my belly's hung up on my backbone."

They got as far as the porch before the older woman turned facing them.

"We'll feed you, but that's all. You understand?"

The soiled, rumpled, tired, beard-stubbled men stared. The older woman went inside followed by the girl. The men trooped in one behind the other.

The women went to work at the cook-stove, the men sat around the table on anything they could find to sit on, and watched. Once the older woman turned and addressed Carter Alvarado. "You'd ought to join Ned Buntline an' write stories. You're a pretty fair liar." She swept her steely look over the others. "If you're posse-riders I'm a Dutchman's uncle," and before any of them could respond she turned back to the stove slamming iron frypans and cooking utensils.

By the time they were fed every man had been inhaling cooking aromas for quite a spell. They didn't remove their hats nor ask where the wash stand was. The older woman watched, pursed her lips and went around the table snatching off hats. Only Mort looked up, and after meeting the woman's hostile glare went back to eating.

She tossed their hats in a corner while the girl refilled cups and did the running and fetching. Near the end of the meal Jake Swindin eased back to fish in a trouser pocket. He met the woman's hostile stare, hung there briefly, removed the hand from his pocket and dredged up a puny smile as he said, "Well, anyway, it was a mighty fine meal, ma'am."

She stood like a wooden Indian until the last cup was emptied then herded them out of the house. Down at the barn she looked at their head-hung, tucked up animals and told the girl to turn them in a back corral. She told Jake to take fresh horses, stood arms crossed as the men brought in ranch animals and went to work rigging out. She had all of them thoroughly cowed. When they were ready to ride and led the horses out of the barn the woman led the way.

John Doyle came over close to the

woman and softly said, "We'll get the horses back to you some way," and held out his closed fist. When she raised her palm he opened his fingers and several gold coins passed between them.

The woman raised a dark look which John Doyle ignored. "Lady, I'm not payin' for the meal nor for the loan of the horses . . . That girl most likely would like a new dress an' a bonnet."

The woman closed her hand around the money. "What do you know about girls?" she snapped.

As John Doyle was swinging astride he answered, "I buried one about her age in Texas six, seven years ago. Good day to you, an' thanks again."

The last rider to depart was Carter Alvarado. He made an elaborate salute to the girl, grinned and rode away. The girl got close to the older woman as she said, "That one's right likely, Ma."

The older woman snorted, took her daughter by the arm and marched to the house. On the porch as she released the girl she said, "Tami, that kind will do nothin' but break your heart." The woman stiffened, head up and facing westerly. There were riders approaching. She said, "Follerin' their tracks. Get inside, girl."

She was right about the tracks. The approaching horsemen were indeed riding parallel to the tracks and there was no way to misinterpret their purpose; they were following the men who had just left the yard.

From the parlour window the woman and girl watched them enter the yard. They ignored the house, tracked right to the barn and swung to the ground.

Moments later a man called, the others trooped out back and lined up outside the pole corral gazing at ridden-down animals eating hay. Each tucked up horse had saddle-mark sweat stains.

There were nine of them, filthy, stained and gaunt. The woman recognized the dark, angry-faced man by his badge, went to the door and called, "Sheriff;

my husband went to Mirage to find you. We heard guns yesterday." She waited for an explanation which she did not get until the fiery-eyed lawman came to the foot of the porch and looked up. "Rustlers an' some drovers who threw in with 'em. How long ago since they got fresh horses and left?"

"Half-hour, maybe a little more." As the woman said this she raised an arm. "They rode into the brakes westerly." She lowered the arm. "They're fresh-mounted."

The disagreeable man had the answer to that. "We'll need fresh mounts too," he told the woman.

Her answer was cryptic. "We only keep six or eight using horses. You're welcome to what's left but there won't be as many as you need."

The sheriff's face darkened. The men with him looked more dispirited than tired, maybe as much of one as the other.

A red-headed man with a bandage

around his head, his hat perched atop it, said, "Mr Baron, I've gone about as far as I can go," and sank down on the bottom step.

A large man looked down derisively. "I told you, Mr Baron, he's not only a lousy scout, he ain't got the bottom for posse ridin'."

The older woman went down beside the redhead, lifted his hat, batted at flies with it and spoke to the lawman without looking up. "Leave this one," she said and arose. She spoke in the same flinty tone of voice she had used to her first visitors this day.

Sheriff Baron cast one disdaining glance at the slumped man with the bandaged head and ignored him. The woman stood straight as a ramrod, arms crossed. She studied the men with the sheriff and said, "Wash rack's around back. Get clean then come to the kitchen."

She re-entered the house where her daughter had been standing at the parlour window. She turned to address the older woman. "They look like renegades; filthy, and armed to the teeth."

Her mother ignored that assessment. "Get the stove fired up, Tami. I wish to Gawd your pa'd get back. I'll set the table."

The girl was at the stove when she said, "I don't think there's enough stew, Ma."

The older woman replied without looking up, "Add two cups of flour, seven cups of water, an' a dab of jerky from the jar."

Before the men trooped in from out back the woman went out front, got the injured man on his feet, led him inside to a bedroom, yanked his boots off and told him to lie back. She barely had time to get a draft of sleeping powders mixed with red wine down him before the remaining posse-riders arrived to be fed.

The sheriff dropped his hat. The others followed this example. As the lawman sat at the table he asked the woman questions. "How many was there, ma'am?"

"Seven."

"Did they say what their destination was?"

"No. They just ate like starved men an' left."

"Did you recognize any of 'em?"

This time the woman raised steely eyes to the sheriff. "I don't recollect ever seein' any of 'em before. What are they wanted for?"

"Rustlin', horse stealin'. There's bounties on 'em."

As the woman placed food and bowls on the table the older woman addressed the lawman. "I got your hurt posseman in a back room. When he's fit I'll see that he gets back to town."

The sheriff nodded around a mouthful of food, but that large, dark-eyed man with a cruel mouth, told the woman how the redheaded man had let himself get trapped and knocked over the head. The speaker's tone sounded as though he enjoyed the injured man's problem.

The woman fixed the large, dark-eyed man with a piercing gaze and said, "How old are you?"

The question was so unexpected most of the eating men paused, forks poised. The large man scowled. "Thirty-five. How old are you, woman?"

"Old enough," she said, standing erectly behind the sheriff's chair, "to know that by the time you're my age you'll have been bloodied like the lad in the back room. I'd guess not once but several times."

She went to the stove to help her daughter lift the cast iron stew pot from a burner to the warmer.

The men at the table did not say a word, but among those who studied the woman's ramrod straight back, was the sheriff.

7

Nightfall

THE grazing country south and west of the ranch had veiny brakes, some deep enough to hide a mounted man and, although Jake and John Doyle had watched the sheriff arrive from just below the rim of one of those brakes, when Jake suggested they sneak back and turn the horses loose as they'd done in the high country, John Doyle shook his head.

There was nothing wrong with the idea and in fact it probably could have been accomplished. They had seen the sheriff and his riders enter the house, something which required no great prescience to encourage a belief food had something to do with it.

John Doyle explained his reason curtly. "They ain't our worry. We got most of the fresh animals. They can't overtake us." As he said this John Doyle reined around to follow the deep arroyo southward. "Our concern is to get as far from that place as we can."

The pair of newly mounted former possemen exchanged a look. They didn't have to know about a man's past to recognize that a man who thought as John Doyle did was experienced in dodging pursuit.

They were still tired but less so now that they were astride fresh animals and had food behind their belts, but ultimately the same dissatisfaction which had encouraged their break with Sheriff Baron began to surface among the former possemen as they followed John Doyle.

He kept to the broken country as much as he could until he was confident they were out of sight of pursuit. What bothered even Alvarado and Jake Swindin was Doyle's sashaying instead of riding in a straight line.

His reason did not become clear

until every one of them was convinced the lawman would by now be following their tracks — the only horse sign although there was an abundance of cattle sign.

He found the creek he had been searching for, rode down the middle of it for close to a mile before handing his reins to Jake so he could climb a crumbly bank and while lying prone, tip down his hat and watch for movement.

Sure enough it was back there, but he scowled. Instead of the nine riders who had entered the ranch yard there were only four.

When he got back to the others and reported what he had seen Carter Alvarado thought aloud. "That's all the fresh animals they could get." He was right, but the sheriff was also accustomed to manhunting. The men he'd had to leave behind had probably been sent to Mirage, a ride their tired animals could make in time.

John Doyle led off again, following

the creek fetlock deep in water until they had dense thickets of creek willows ahead, beyond which, eastward, there was timber.

Orville told Carter there'd still be muddy water when the pursuit reached the creek, and Alvarado shrugged as they fought their way through creek willows into the timber beyond.

Here, they rode toward higher ground and halted to blow the horses in a little grassy place. Alvarado walked back to watch the back trail, and got a surprise. The pursuing riders had clearly been pushing their fresh animals; they were less than a couple of miles northward and making good time.

He went back to tell Swindin and Doyle that the ruse of riding in running water wasn't going to help. The sheriff's party would find disturbed silt before it could be washed clear by running water.

John Doyle considered the area, decided it was adequate for an ambush, and suggested places where his companions could conceal themselves because, for a fact, that hard-riding lawman would follow their tracks right uphill easterly from the creek.

His final words were: "Four or five — we can get around 'em. We got dang near double their number."

Orville had a question. "What'll we do with 'em?"

No one answered as the men led their horses among timber on both sides of the trail they had made uphill from the creek, but where Carter finally halted to tie his horse Orville asked it again, and this time he got an answer. "Take 'em back to Mirage tied like shoats."

The reason Orville had asked the question came out when he replied. "That's their town, Carter. If we ride in down there herdin' their lawman an' his riders, I'll give you good odds we'll be hangin' from trees."

Alvarado, who had been listening for the pursuit, slowly faced around. The skinny man was right. *They* were the

132

wanted men, not the sheriff or his possemen. He looked for John Doyle but could not find him. He told Orville to watch the trail and struck out for the little meadow. When he reached it he called loudly for John Doyle.

The answer he got was not from John Doyle, it was from Jake Swindin who did not move where Alvarado could see him when he said, "They ain't comin' up here. Doyle went out to scout 'em. They stopped where we come out of the creek, looked up the slope then continued on southward. Doyle's farther down watchin' 'em."

Alvarado returned to the place where he and the skinny man had a fair view of the lower country. They did not see John Doyle but sure enough, their pursuers were riding south-westerly, the direction of Mirage.

Carter led his horse to where Orville was and related what he had been told. The skinny man said, "I got a hunch. Them four won't go as far as town, they'll fan out somewhere southerly an' wait for us to come along. An' the others'll be patrollin' the country watchin' in case we ride in a different direction."

Alvarado listened to this, swung for a final look southward where their pursuers were small in the distance, swung back toward Orville Bean about the time a moving shadow appeared.

John Doyle was rumpled. He looked tired as he eased down on a deadfall gazing at Alvarado and the skinny man. "It'd help if I knew the sheriff. I could maybe figure how he thinks."

Orville repeated what he had told Alvarado and John Doyle nodded. "Somethin' like that. Whoever was ramroddin' that bunch that bypassed us smelled an ambush sure as I'm settin' here." Doyle stood up. "Let's get a-horseback, gents. We got to do some figurin'."

When they arrived in the clearing Jake and the others came from behind large trees. Swindin asked where the pursuers were and when John Doyle told him the drover stood like stone. "It don't make sense, them chasin' us up in here, then ridin' on."

John Doyle did not respond, he told them all to get mounted and as he was preparing to do the same the turncoat named Alf approached and said, "If the sheriff wasn't with that bunch, my guess is that he went straight south some miles west of here where him an' a feller named Cogswell more'n likely got them stampeded cattle holed up."

John Doyle swung astride and while evening his reins he gazed at the former posse-rider. "Are you sayin' the sheriff an' another feller is in the cattle-stealin' business?"

Alf's reply held all the mounted men within hearing still and silent. "No, as far as I know they never stole cattle, but I've seen what happened north of town happen other times when cattle drives come up through this country. They get stampeded. Cogswell and his sons gather in all they can."

John Doyle fixed Alf with a cold

stare. "An' that ain't cattle stealin'?"

Alf gave Doyle look for look. "It ain't cattle stealin'. If you'll shut up I'll tell you why."

John Doyle nodded in silence.

The man who had changed sides with Alf stared steadily at his companion without speaking. His expression implied disapproval of what Alf was explaining.

Alf did not look in his partner's direction, his attention was on John Doyle when he continued speaking. "Cogswell an' his boys does everythin' legal. They round up drover cattle, send word they got 'em, an' when drover or an owner shows up they hand him a bill for the cattle. When they complain the sheriff reads 'em the law about what he calls impound."

Jake Swindin interrupted. "How do you know all this?"

Alf answered matter-of-factly. "Me'n him'n a lot of other fellers around Mirage been paid to find loose cattle an' drive 'em to the Cogswell place. Plumb legal, Mr Swindin."

A few heads nodded among the band of riders. Alf added a clincher. "Henry Cogswell's done real well over the years ransomin' cattle back to their owners."

Alf's companion who had been silent up to now, finally spoke. "Them as won't pay or can't pay Cogswell an' the sheriff take cattle instead. Nothin' illegal Cliff Baron told me. Drovers lose drifters all the time."

Orville Bean sounded indignant when he said, "Stampeded cattle ain't the same as cut-outs an' drifters."

No one argued; John Doyle put a bemused look on Jake Swindin. "I expect there's more'n one way to skin a cat." He returned his attention to Alf. "Can you take us to this Cogswell place?'

Alf nodded, reined toward the downhill path and did not stop until they had recrossed the creek. When John Doyle and Jake Swindin paused to await the crossing of the others Alf rode up and said, "If that's where the sheriff went I expect there'll be watchers."

John Doyle gestured for Alf to lead off and the others followed. It required time for Alf's revelation to soak in among the men who hadn't already known about the ransom-for-cattle scheme. John Doyle asked Jake if he'd ever lost cattle before in the Mirage country. Jake could not give a definitive reply. "A big drive like this one just naturally loses a few head along the way. If you mean was I ever stampeded in this country before, the answer is no." Swindin briefly brightened. "But there's always a first time, ain't there?"

John Doyle was quiet and thoughtful for a solid hour and meanwhile the terrain subtly changed. There now were occasional spits of trees, mostly soft wood but with an infrequent bosque of oaks, and what had heretofore been broken or undulating grassland country became as flat as a man's hand, and when John Doyle finally broke his silence it was to dourly comment on his riders crossing country where they stood out like peas shaken out of a pod.

John Doyle asked Alf how far the Cogswell place was and got a sweeping gesture along with the answer. "'Nother couple of miles before we get on the old man's land an' from there maybe four, five miles before we see the building."

Doyle was impressed. "Does Cogswell run cattle?"

"As many as him'n his two boys can handle. In markin' season he hires a few more fellers." Alf made a dour smile. "One thing — he's always got a lot of cattle."

Jake Swindin dryly commented, "I expect he does have."

John Doyle's reason for asking about distances was that although the day was wearing along, he'd needed reassurance he and his riders would not be visible to watchers. At the distances Alf had stated they would not have to worry about discovery providing they did not pick up their gait. Sundown would arrive before they reached their destination.

Orville spoke aloud to no one in particular when he said, "If the sheriff's up there, an' if Cogswell has maybe more than just his boys, an' if them fellers we tried to bushwhack is also up there, we're likely to be out-numbered to beat hell, ain't we?"

John Doyle replied but not for a while, and when he did he twisted to look at the skinny man whom he had hardly considered before.

"If they don't know we're comin' we got a fair chance."

Carter Alvarado and Jake exchanged a look. John Doyle had, over time, revealed himself to be a knowledgeable outlaw, not just a commonplace outlaw.

The taciturn man who rode with Alf dug out several sticks of jerky from his saddle-bag, kept one for himself and passed the other sticks around. It wasn't much but it sure-Lord beat deep breathing as an appetite suppressant.

This man and Alf engaged in an

undertone discussion which did not last long. The others noticed and inevitably suspicion about those two surfaced but nothing was said. In fact the men riding with Jake Swindin were about as unique an assortment of riders as a man could imagine.

Carter Alvarado shook his head. What had started out as a simple cattle drive had turned into something no one who heard about it would believe, an honest drover riding with professional rustlers and possemen who had switched sides from being manhunters of the others to being their partners in a venture that now appeared headed for a show-down with a mean lawman and someone most of them had never heard of before — Henry Cogswell — who in association with a sheriff, worked a scheme for getting rich off other folks' livestock without actually stealing them.

An hour later with the sun balancing atop some distant peaks dusk arrived. Two hours later Alf changed course, led the way atop a landswell where they sat with loose reins looking ahead where lights shone faintly from buildings. Alf said, "That's the Cogswell place."

Orville had a question. "How handy is these Cogswells?"

Alf replied without looking around. "Handy enough I expect. I've never heard of 'em fightin' but to be safe it wouldn't hurt to figure they will." Alf twisted to face the skinny man. "I can tell you for a fact: Sheriff Baron's real handy."

That subject was allowed to die after Alvarado made a dry remark. "We ain't settin' out here because we figure we're goin' to a church social."

Alf swung to the ground and while standing with his horse, trailing one rein, he gestured. Lowing cattle could be heard in the distance, not distraught animals, livestock seeking companions at a bedding ground. With this distant background noise Alf told John Doyle it might be a good idea to ride completely across the range and approach the buildings from the west. His idea was that if the sheriff was down there and if Cogswell had been told what had happened in the high country, there would be watchers out in the night, most probably listening for horsemen approaching from either the east or north. If they got far enough westerly, then came in from the west Alf thought, they just might be able to effect a surprise.

Again Alf led off. Even with night falling he seemed to know the route and he went far south before turning northerly then sashaying westerly.

As far as any of them thought, their presence had not been discovered. Once, they started some bedded-down cattle to their feet. They were so close Jake did not even lean to look but began swearing while sitting straight up in his saddle. The cattle wore both the large star brand of their owner, Alonzo Starr, and Jake Swindin's road mark.

Carter Alvarado trailed John Doyle who trailed Alf. Lights at the house firmed up into square shapes and eventually the dark and bulky outline of buildings became discernible. At about the same time a dog sat back and barked furiously. Two of the lights went out. One in the rear of the house remained bright.

Orville cursed the dog which kept up its racket even after Alf halted and John Doyle quietly spoke. "In their boots I'd expect it's men out here not bears or coyotes."

Someone lighted a lamp in a square, small log building. John Doyle made a correct guess about that. "Bunkhouse." He looked at Alf. "Cogswell an' his two boys run things?"

Alf answered dryly. "Not if the sheriff an' his friends got here ahead of us, an' maybe Cogswell's got some other fellers to help him round up the cattle. I got no idea how many's there."

The bunkhouse door opened, a large, beefy man was briefly framed in the light before he closed the door. John Doyle dismounted and gestured for

144

the others to do the same. The bulky man called the dog and the barking stopped.

Carter wanted to make the scout. John Doyle nodded without speaking and Alvarado left the others and within moments was out of sight. Jake turned to John Doyle. "How good is he?"

"Good enough," Doyle replied as they all stood at the head of their horses to prevent nickering, and waited. Orville muttered something about the number of men likely to be opposing them, which annoyed John Doyle because he answered sharply, "Leave if you're of a mind."

That effectively silenced the skinny man. None of the others spoke, they listened and waited.

The beefy individual went back into the bunkhouse. There was a glow of yellow light as he opened and closed the door. He may have taken the dog with him, at any rate it did not resume its barking.

Carter reappeared — from the

south — and surprised the men who had been watching westerly. He had something with him which he dumped at Jake Swindin's feet. It was part of a green hide with the brands clearly visible, the star mark and the Swindin road brand which was a simple small mark in the shape of the spade used in card games.

Jake groaned. They had butchered one of the Starr animals. Carter said it was hanging on a corral. Whoever cut the marked skin out most likely figured to bury or burn it.

John Doyle barely glanced at the piece of hide, he was interested in how close Alvarado had got and what he had seen.

Carter's reply was cryptic. "There's a corral full of saddle stock an' another four or five head stalled in the barn." Alvarado added a little more. "If they got watchers out, they're either distant from the barn or asleep."

John Doyle asked again about the horses and Alvarado answered shortly.

"As near as I could count, six or eight in the corral. It could be nine, I didn't spend time countin'."

John Doyle let out a loud breath. "Four in the barn could be the fellers who chased us. If it's nine in the corral that'll be the sheriff an' them as rode with him."

Alvarado said, "I didn't see no watchers, but I wouldn't bet they ain't out here. I think I can get back an' chouse the horses out of the corral."

Orville Bean volunteered to accompany Alvarado. Jake eyed the skinny man with an expression that was invisible in darkness. His opinion of the skinny man was that he lacked the 'bottom' for what he'd volunteered for.

John Doyle nodded for Carter and Orville to leave, and as soon as they were lost in darkness he told the others to follow him into the yard, but first to make sure the horses were tied. That business of setting folks afoot he knew from experience was a boot that fitted both feet.

As they began stalking it bothered Jake that the dog didn't start raising hell again and propping it up.

When they were close enough John Doyle set Alf and his reticent companion to watch the bunkhouse. He told them if anyone tried to come outside they were to shoot, "Close enough to scare 'em back inside," then he led the others in a roundabout way toward the main house.

The only time they froze was when a man emerged from the main house to pee. They waited for the man to go back inside, but he took his time.

After he had returned inside several lamps were relighted.

8

Doing the Right Thing

JOHN DOYLE'S plan seemed to be to capture those at the main house by surprise, which troubled more than Jake Swindin. They were not only outnumbered but as they stalked the house there were those men behind them at the bunkhouse.

The same anxiety bothered Alvarado. Orville worried too but he was a natural worrier.

They made a big sashay to get behind the main house. By the time they got close back to there Jake was sweating. They could hear men talking inside. To Jake it sounded like an awful lot of them.

He edged close to John Doyle to speak when someone flung open a rear door, stepped out on to the porch, reset his hat and marched down off the porch right into the arms of the stalkers. His surprise was total, otherwise he might have yelped. John Doyle disarmed the man, spun him half around and asked how many were inside. The man may not have been frightened, but he certainly was surprised. Without hesitation he said, "Fifteen or sixteen."

Jake's heart nearly stopped. Not a word was said for several seconds after which John Doyle asked if the sheriff was in there. The captive nodded vigorously.

"An' Henry Cogswell?"

Another vigorous nod.

John Doyle spoke curtly. "What I'd like is to get 'em out here one or two at a time."

The captive was silent.

"What's your name?"

"Terry Cogswell."

"The old man's son?"

"Yes."

"Terry, you expect you could get

150

your pa an' brother out here?"

"How?"

"That's up to you," John Doyle said and cocked his Colt.

Cogswell licked his lips without taking his eyes off John Doyle. "I'll call to 'em. Others might come too."

John Doyle took young Cogswell by the arm to the porch, told him to open the door and call out. Cogswell obeyed, moved aside leaving the door open, and when an older bearded man appeared followed by a rawboned younger man, John Doyle allowed them to get past the doorway. The bearded man had a question. "What is it, boy?"

If the overhang hadn't precluded good visibility the older man could have seen Terry's expression. He did not see it nor did Terry answer because John Doyle spoke quietly with his back to the closed door. "Hands atop your heads, gents, and walk straight forward."

The older man looked at Terry, hoisted both hands and moved down off the porch. His elder son followed the older man's example in stony silence, but the venomous look he threw his brother spoke volumes.

Jake saw them coming, unshipped his handgun and as each captive passed he emptied their holsters and flung the weapons out into the night.

John Doyle took them out a-ways where it was no longer possible to hear talking inside the house, leathered his six-gun and studied the Cogswells over a period of silence, before he addressed the older man. "What's your name?"

"Henry Cogswell. What's yours?"

Doyle's hand was a blur but when it connected with Henry Cogswell's face the sound was loud enough. The rawboned Cogswell started to lunge. Jake shoved out a foot. The elder Cogswell's son went down in a cursing sprawl. When he regained his feet he glared at Swindin.

Henry Cogswell spoke to his big, rawboned son. "Leave it be."

John Doyle told Cogswell he wanted

the sheriff, and the bearded man snorted. "Walk in there an' get him," he said.

John Doyle smiled thinly. "Let's see if you can call him out like Terry done you."

Old Cogswell glared. One of his sons was belligerent, the younger one wasn't. The old man looked at his elder son, who slowly shook his head. The old man nodded agreement. Swindin was beginning to get edgy. He told John Doyle they were wasting time. Doyle did not comment but moments later he jerked his head for the captives to be herded down the west side of the house. When they reached the corner Doyle peeked around. The lighted bunkhouse was the nearest building. Beyond it was the barn. He said, "Around behind the bunkhouse."

They got about half the distance when someone up ahead cocked a gun. They stopped stone still. John Doyle called softly. "Alvarado?"

"Naw. Orville." The skinny man had

153

recognized Doyle's voice. "Who you got there?"

Doyle did not answer. "Where's Carter?"

"'Round front somewhere."

"Keep watch," Doyle said, and growled at the Cogswells, who continued in the direction of the barn. When they got there John Doyle stopped them at the wide, doorless rear opening. It was as dark inside as the bottom of a well.

With a man on each side the Cogswells were taken inside. The only sound was when the younger Cogswell looked at his guard and said, "Mort!"

The reply was brusquely given. "Yeah. Me'n Alf."

Mort might have said more but someone hissed for silence.

Jake looked around for John Doyle. They were midway along the barn runway and had stopped. What they would do with their captives worried him.

John Doyle resolved Jake's anxiety by

ordering the Cogswells tied and gagged. There was some resistance but it was handily overcome. Searching for rope in a dark barn might have produced something desirable if someone hadn't stumbled over some light chain.

They chained the Cogswells at the ankle, with both arms made fast in back and used the Cogswells' own bandannas to muffle them. The rawboned one writhed and swore through his gag but the old man seemed resigned. With eyes accustomed to the gloom he watched John Doyle the way a hawk would watch a snake.

The men were near the saddle pole where John Doyle meant to palaver, when all hell broke loose somewhere in the general direction of the bunkhouse.

It started with one shot which quickly became a veritable fusillade. Someone yelled, there was a lull then the gunfire brisked up again.

Jake said something the others could not make out as John Doyle headed out the doorless wide rear opening.

The others followed.

There was another lull in the gunfire. For about ten seconds there was nothing but echoes until a man called gruffly, "Clint? You over there?"

Whoever Clint was he did not answer.

The silence drew out until someone made a loud grunt as he fell and arose swearing. John Doyle made a sound-shot which either found a target or came awfully close because a man squawked and ran. His running was audible in the lengthening lull.

The men with John Doyle could hear men moving. Mort said, "The barn!"

But John Doyle did not turn back. He and his companions were not strong enough, nor possibly foolish enough, to brace their enemies, without the four log walls of a barn, where the tactic of engagement was simple; with shotguns the barn's interior could be sluiced, with handguns the same thing could happen.

Orville Bean came sprinting like a

stork, knees almost as high as his chest. Alf tackled him. Orville fought like a sow bear until Jake came over and growled. As Orville stopped resisting Alf helped him to his feet and Orville said "It's a damned army."

Someone by the bunkhouse called. "Henry? Henry, we got one. You out here? Henry?"

Jake swore under his breath. They had Carter Alvarado. Westerly, some distance behind John Doyle's companions, someone cut loose with a scattergun. They saw muzzleblast and heard pellets but evidently the range was too great because no one was hit, but with men behind them and on both sides as well as over in front of the bunkhouse, Orville's exclamation about an army got credibility.

Jake leaned to tell John Doyle they had better get back to the horses, and Doyle nodded as he led off northward where they got some protection among some outbuildings before Doyle altered course heading for the area where they had tied their animals.

The gunfire had ended, as had John Doyle's plan of capturing their enemies one and two at a time, which may not have been possible in any event, but if there was an alternative strategy none of them knew what it was.

As they made stealthy progress toward their animals Jake Swindin decided John Doyle's intention had been of the best, but his chance of succeeding against such odds now seemed to Jake to have been foolhardy.

Back in the yard there was a light in the barn. The Cogswells had been found, and as sure as the good Lord made sour apples they had told their friends what had happened, how it had happened and how few attackers there were.

None of the retreating men spoke. As with Jake, they nursed disillusionment in silence. Whatever might have happened, didn't, and what was left was get clear of the Cogswell place as far and as fast as they could.

Jake abruptly threw out an arm and stopped. For a moment no one moved. What had stopped Jake was the horses, visible but just barely. They were not looking in the direction of their riders, they were standing alert, heads up and little ears pointing northward.

John Doyle sighed. It sounded loud in the deathly hush. Orville whispered. "They found the horses."

Someone growled the skinny man into silence.

John Doyle looked around, selected the least talkative among them and sent him to scout. After he had blended with the night his companion, Alf, barely more than whispered when he told John Doyle he'd picked the best man for night-hunting. Alf did not elaborate and Jake did not even look at the speaker. He was watching the horses.

Orville got jumpy. Alternately he watched the horses and back the way they had come. It seemed to him that their enemies would guess they were no longer in the yard and would — correctly — assume they were making for their horses.

Maybe others did not like hunkering like squaws in the dark, waiting, but that too was something no one mentioned, nor would it have been necessary to mention.

Eventually John Doyle arose. The others, assuming he had seen the returning scout, also arose.

A man spoke without raising his voice, and it wasn't Mort. He said, "Set still, gents. Real still. Don't start somethin' you can't finish . . . Now then, the guns, pitch 'em away, stand up with your hands atop your heads."

John Doyle did not move, nor did his companions. The next time they were spoken to from out in the darkness somewhere, the voice was gruff and came from the west, behind them.

"Do like the man said. You got half a minute. You're plumb surrounded. *Stand up an' shed them weapons!*"

Alf swore with feeling, pitched his

weapon away and stood Up. Orville was the next. The last man was John Doyle.

Their gruff-voiced captor called out. "We got 'em, Clint."

The milder voice replied almost indifferently. "All right. We'll lead the horses back."

Gruff-voice came into view with three men whose handguns were aimed and cocked. Gruff-voice stopped to consider his captives. He knew two of them and said, "We figured you'n Mort had quit an' headed for town."

Alf said nothing but his taciturn partner did. "You're on the wrong side, Hennessey."

The gruff-voiced man's reply was given with conviction. "I don't think so, Mort. We got the law on our side."

The man with the calm voice who had not become visible spoke again. "Start 'em back, Hennessey, we'll follow with the horses."

Hennessey gestured for the captives

161

to start walking in the direction of the yard. For some time he and his companions walked in stony silence. Orville broke the hush by reproachfully asking one of their guards why in the name of Gawd he still rode with Sheriff Baron.

The answer he got would have surprised no one who knew the mental limitations of the man who gave it. "I'm on the side of the law," the man stated. "Folks got to have law."

When they reached the yard there were lights in the main house. The number of their captors had been increasing on the walk. In the yard were other men. Tied to a chair on the skimpy little bunkhouse porch was Carter Alvarado. He said nothing nor did anyone address him as the captives were herded toward the main house.

The light was blinding, not just to the captives, but the snarling voice which reached them did not require recognition. Henry Cogswell's indignation was obvious. "You sons of bitches tied up the wrong men. When it gets lighter me'n my boys'll lean on the ropes in the barn — maybe."

A greying man slightly to one side of Cogswell put a long look on the bearded man, turned in the direction of the kitchen and stiffened a cup of coffee from a bottle. Eventually he returned to the parlour but did not enter it; he stood in the doorway.

A stocky, dark man pushed through to face the captives. "Stealin' horses is hangin' business. Shootin' at lawmen's even worse." The sheriff fixed his malevolent glare on Mort and his partner. "You double-crossin' bastards, you takin' the sides of them two standin' beside you makes you renegades. You're goin' to wish you never was born."

Alf looked the sheriff straight in the eye. "Mr Baron, if anyone's got a hangin' comin' it's not us. If them federal marshals knew about you'n Mr Cogswell an' how you're sellin' drovers' cattle back to 'em, they'd . . . "

Sheriff Baron launched himself with a snarl, Alf tried to step clear but one of their captors was in the way.

John Doyle took only two steps, caught the sheriff by the coat and swung from the shoulder. The blow did not land squarely but it knocked the lawman down. A cruel-faced large man helped the sheriff to his feet, but the lawman was unsteady so the large man elbowed him aside and started forward.

The man leaning in the kitchen doorway drew his six-gun and fired into the ceiling. All activity stopped. He holstered his gun and said, "That's enough. Lock 'em away until daylight so's we can figure what to do with 'em."

The prisoners were taken to a storeroom and shoved inside. The door was locked from the outside. Jake Swindin groped the four walls with both hands. It was dark, there were no windows and what little light came from beneath the door was no more than a sliver.

Orville said, "Nice. Real nice."

Jake grunted from the darkness. John Doyle felt his way to the wall. There was a narrow slit, boarded up and evidently latched from the outside. It was the exact height for men to unload wagons through the small opening. It was also too high in the wall for the men inside to get high enough to break it open.

While they were examining what appeared to be a granary door someone rammed a key into the door and turned it. Light came in but not blindingly, and the men near the back wall watched a slow, humourless smile spread across the face of that large, cruel-mouthed man. He did not enter the room but remained in the doorway as he said, "You'll never get the thing opened. Henry spiked timbers across it from the outside years back. Which one of you is Swindin?"

Jake stepped away from the back wall. "I am."

The large man jerked his head. "They

want to talk to you." As Jake left the room the large man said, "Go ahead, try bustin' it open," laughed, closed and locked the door and herded Jake into the parlour.

There were expressionless faces with hostile eyes in the parlour. The sheriff and Henry Cogswell were sitting on chairs side by side. The sheriff spoke sharply to Jake. "I'm goin' to kill that son of a bitch." Before Jake could respond Cogswell held up a hand. Standing behind the older man's chair was his stone-faced, rawboned, elder son.

Cogswell addressed Jake Swindin in a calm voice. "Mister, Alonzo Starr ain't goin' to like what you done — running his cattle over our winter feed like you owned the countryside."

Jake felt for a chair and sat down.

"I'll tell you why he ain't goin' to like it — because his cattle done a lot of damage, an' us local stockmen count on that graze to get us through the winter, an' Mr Swindin, now we'll have

166

to sell down to stay in business. You understand what I'm tellin' you?"

Jake said, "I'm listenin'."

Cogswell leaned slightly in his chair staring at Jake. "You fixed it so's we'll have to sell cows, replacement heifers and some bulls. Mr Swindin, I'm goin' to be in a very bad way now that you've spoilt our winter feed. An' Mr Starr's goin' to have to pay in full to get his cattle back."

Jake sighed and loosened in the chair, still silent.

"It's the law, Mr Swindin. Mostly, them cattle run over my range. I'll have to sell way down come autumn. Way down. Not through anythin' I done. You understand what I'm gettin' at?"

Jake woodenly nodded still silent. What Cogswell was saying was that he had ruined Jake Swindin. He would never be hired again to drive cattle.

"Well now, Mr Swindin, suppose we come to an agreement about this. I'll figure it out, give it to you on paper an' you go to the telegraph in Mirage an' send a message to Mr Starr. You can do that? Because if you can't, why then I'll have to take other steps, under the law you understand. Everythin' I've said is accordin' to the law. You can ask the sheriff if it ain't."

Jake gazed at the dark, disagreeable lawman who glared back. "Impoundin' to satisfy a debt is legal."

Cogswell made his final statement. "Them fellers who come skulkin' here in the night figurin' to shoot some of us, the sheriff'll take them to town, lock 'em up an' when the circuit ridin' judge gets here in a week or two, the sheriff'll have wrote out the charges. Horse-stealin', attempted murder an' robbery, cattle stealin' an' trespassin'. Mr Swindin, I'm tryin' to be reasonable about all this, you tryin' to kill me'n my boys, shootin' up the yard; them things got to be figured in the bill to Mr Starr."

That tall man leaning in the kitchen doorway was gazing at Jake. He seemed to be amused. Jake was sure he had never seen the man before, but there were other men in the room; Sheriff Baron's posse-riders from Mirage, he had never seen before either.

"Mr Swindin . . . ?"

Jake's weariness made him slow in answering. "I'll send the message to Mr Starr."

Cogswell's grave expression brightened. He arose and spoke to his sons. "Rassle somethin' for Mr Swindin an' his friends to eat. The sheriff an' me'll be in my office figurin' things." He turned back toward Jake. "You're doin' the right thing."

9

Springing the Trap

TERRY COGSWELL was an excellent cook. The meal he made for the captives was as good as any of them had ever eaten. Their abrupt change from prisoners in a dark room to freed men being fed, even joked with a little, had to have been achieved at a price. None of them asked questions until they were rigging out in the barn and Jake sidled close to Carter Alvarado to explain. Carter leaned across his saddle seat looking at Jake. The older man misinterpreted the look and said, "I didn't have no choice", and walked over to rig out his own animal.

As Orville had said earlier, it was an army, a small one but an impressive one that left the Cogswell yard with dawn breaking. It was cold and dawnlight was never very uplifting, not until the sun arrived.

Sheriff Baron rode with several hard-faced men, Henry Cogswell left the yard riding stirrup with Jake Swindin. Behind them were Orville, John Doyle, Carter Alvarado, Davy Twigs and the men who had changed sides. These individuals were treated roughly by their captors. Several times Alf would have answered back but Mort shook his head. 'Accidents' happened.

Jake had been fed, had emptied a cup of black joe laced with whiskey. He was still dog tired and his sense of failure began increasing long before they had Mirage's rooftops in sight. He told Henry Cogswell he doubted very much that Alonzo Starr would pay as much as Cogswell wanted, and got an easy answer accompanied by a crafty smile. "It'll be fine with me if he don't. For every day his cattle are on my range he'll have to pay, which means if he don't pony up, I just might end up ownin' all his cattle. It's the law, Mr Swindin. Some days after he's notified what he owes if he don't pony up, I advertise in the *Mirage Journal*, an' ten days after that if he ain't paid up, title to the cattle passes to me."

Cogswell twisted to face the sheriff. The disagreeable dark man nodded at Jake. "Ten days an' the cattle will belong to Mr Cogswell."

No one spoke for a considerable distance, John Doyle and his riders were sorting out what Alf had explained to them. One or two of them — probably Orville — would conclude that Henry Cogswell and the sheriff were very *coyote* individuals and while not liking them would be impressed by their craftiness.

Mirage was a pretty village, folks tended their gardens, there was a white-painted school and Methodist church. There were several businesses including the customary mercantile establishment, a large building with a genuine glass window that the proprietor covered each night with steel shutters.

The jailhouse, originally a log granary, had been sided over with planed lumber. Sheriff Baron led off and dismounted in front, looped his reins at the tie rack and without a look around unlocked the thick roadside door, stood aside and scowled as he jerked his head for John Doyle and his companions to enter.

The last man in was Mort; as he passed the lawman he growled something the others did not hear but which the sheriff heard and when Mort's back was turned, clubbed him from behind over the head with his six-gun barrel.

Alf started for the sheriff, who cocked his weapon and said, "Try it, you traitorous son of a bitch. Try it!"

John Doyle caught Alf by the arm and swung him, pushed him backwards until he stumbled against a wall bench and sat down.

Baron put up his Colt glared and left

the jail-house. They heard him lock up from the outside.

Alvarado went to the empty gunrack and afterwards rummaged in the sheriff's desk. He found several cartons of bullets, even charges for a shotgun, which were worthless without the weapons.

Alf and Jake got Mort to a bench near a hanging *olla* from which they got water to wash the bleeding scalp wound. Mort responded neither to questions nor the sting when his torn scalp was being doctored.

He was almost half an hour coming back to normal. When they told him how he had been clubbed, Mort did not say a word. He studied the empty gun rack, ransacked the desk, got up and drank deeply from the *olla*.

Henry Cogswell and Sheriff Baron came for Jake. Mort's eyes never left the sheriff, even after the door was closed and locked he still stared in that direction.

Mirage was a busy town. The

telegrapher was as skinny and juiceless as a tick, and older than dirt, but he knew his business. When he lowered his head to copy the message Henry Cogswell had handed him Jake saw the bluish tinge the eyeshade gave his face.

The telegrapher read the note twice, copied it word for word on a yellow pad, reversed the pad and handed Cogswell the pen. "Sign at the bottom," he said, and while this was being done the telegrapher studied Jake and the others. He showed no expression as he retrieved the signed pad and turned toward his telegraph key. He asked Cogswell if he expected an answer. Cogswell nodded his head. The telegrapher then said, "If this feller's in Laramie, you can maybe get an answer in an hour. If he ain't, if he's at his ranch or store, whatever he does for a livin', it might take longer. Are you fixin' to stay in town?"

Cogswell smiled. "For as long as it

takes. I just want to be real certain he gets it."

The telegrapher adjusted his blue eyeshade and said, "He'll get it."

They went to the café, settled along the counter and were served coffee. Until Cogswell's eldest son spoke there was silence. He said, "Mr Swindin, do you know this feller Alonzo Starr?"

"I expect so. We palavered three, four times before we come to an agreement about me takin' the drive north."

"Would you say from what you seen of him he'll pay up?"

Jake answered thoughtfully. "I got no idea. I think he can if he is of a mind to. My impression of Mr Starr is that he's a real successful cow man."

"Otherwise you don't know much about him?"

"No sir, I don't." Jake replied, was briefly silent then added a little more. "I think he's some kind of a 'breed. Pretty dark."

They led their animals to the livery barn. The proprietor was another townsman who was expressionless as he and his day man took the animals. After Henry Cogswell went north in the direction of the jailhouse, the liveryman went as far as the wide opening of his establishment. Up there he wagged his head slightly and told his hostler there was something going on sure as day followed night. The day man said nothing.

At the jailhouse Terry Cogswell said he was out of tobacco and struck out in the direction of the emporium. That quiet, greying man who had shot into the ceiling at the Cogswell house watched the youngest Cogswell disappear inside the store. He shrugged slightly and entered the jailhouse with the others. His name was Kent Rogers. He had been riding for the Cogswells for several months. He had proved himself to be a top hand but rarely spoke unless he had to.

The sheriff roared at the sight of his ransacked desk. Old Cogswell ignored him to consider his prisoners. When the sheriff's tirade ended the old man said, "Lock 'em up, Mr Baron."

As the angry sheriff growled for the prisoners to enter his cell room only one man hung back. Mort's bloody shirt and clotted scalp made him stand out. As he shuffled toward the door Sheriff Baron punched him over the kidney from behind. The result was instantaneous and violent. Mort's shuffling gait changed. He turned, stepped sideways and lashed out. Sheriff Baron was caught squarely in the chest by the blow. He staggered. Mort went after him like a catamount. Before the sheriff's companions could interfere, Mort struck the lawman twice more, once in the soft parts and when the sheriff doubled over the second fist caught him under the ear. He went face down.

They came at Mort from several directions. He set his back to the cell room door and snarled defiance. John Doyle and Alvarado turned back in support, but there was no fight, that greying man fired into the ceiling as he'd done out yonder. Everyone stopped. The greying man gestured with his six-gun for the prisoners to continue on into the cell room, and as they turned to obey, the greying man said, "Cogswell, go lock 'em in," and holstered his six-gun. The old man's eldest son followed the prisoners, locked them in and returned to find his father and the greying man working over the sheriff. The old man looked daggers at the greying man. "Don't you never interfere again. You hear me?"

The greying man nodded, rolled the sheriff on to his back and said for someone to fetch a dipper full of water. He dumped the water over the sheriff's face and when he began to splutter Rogers lifted him by the armpits, sat him in his chair at the desk and stepped clear to wipe his hands.

The old man put a narrowed gaze on him. Sheriff Baron was a stocky, heavy man. Rogers had handled him as though he were a child.

The old man took his eldest son over by the gunrack and addressed him in a lowered voice. "I'm beginning to wonder about Kent," he said.

His son scoffed. "Wonder what? He stopped a maulin' like he done at home. Nothin' wrong with that."

"But he's workin' for us."

The rawboned man scowled at his father, turned as someone entered from out front and walked toward his brother to ask if Terry'd got some tobacco. The younger Cogswell handed his brother a sack of Bull Durham with wheat straw papers attached and stared wide eyed at the drenched lawman. "What happened to him?" he asked. No one answered. His older brother lighted up, exhaled and handed back the makings as he lowered his voice to say, "The way this is workin', we're likely to be stuck in town maybe until the mornin'."

Sheriff Baron looked like a drowned rat. He mopped his face, would not trade stares with the others, brought forth a bottle from a lower desk drawer, took down two large swallows and pushed the bottle to the desk's edge. For moments no one reached for it but after one man did the others waited for the bottle to be passed.

The sheriff took Henry Cogswell to the store-room and angrily said this time their ransoming business was being more troublesome than the others had been and he needed a bigger slice of the ransom. Old Cogswell did not turn a hair. He patted the lawman lightly on the shoulder and assured him when they got the money he would increase the sheriff's share, then returned to the office to take a couple more swallows from the depleted bottle.

It was late afternoon when the juiceless telegrapher came looking for Henry Cogswell. He and his companions had recently returned from the café. The scrawny man with the blue eyeshade handed Cogswell a yellow piece of paper and stood like a statue until it had been read before saying, "Any answer?"

Cogswell shook his head, handed the telegrapher half a cartwheel, closed the door after him and read the telegram aloud.

"Best I can do is half what you are asking for damages. If you accept telegram me. Tell Jake Swindin to get the drive started. I will be waiting."

Sheriff Baron sputtered. Henry Cogswell held up a hand. "That figure we come up with last night, I doubled it."

The sheriff stared. Cogswell grinned. "We done that before, Cliff, you'd ought to remember."

The sheriff wasn't finished. "You telegraph him back for the money."

Cogswell nodded. "I will, but by stage it'll be three, four days gettin' here." Cogswell stopped grinning. "We got your jailhouse full of prisoners three, four days they got to be fed an' all."

Sheriff Baron put a hand to his chest. "Not me. I got my sheriffin' to do. Take 'em back to the ranch. There's enough fellers to wet nurse 'em."

Cogswell sank back down on his bench. Other times there had been delays getting money, but this was the first time prisoners were involved. He had a momentary sensation of unease. His eldest son said, "Pa, you got an idea? If you ain't we better get a-horseback an' take 'em home with us. Nothin' else to do. For a fact we dassn't leave 'em here. Locked up or not, we can't take a chance." He faced the sheriff. "Me'n my pa'll go send that telegraph about the money. When we get back have 'em ready to ride."

Henry left the jailhouse with his son. On the stroll to the telegraph office the old man listened to his son and agreed, but not happily. He did not like the idea of having a band of hostile prisoners on his home place, nothing like this had ever happened before. The old man exchanged a curt nod with the telegrapher, scribbled on the yellow pad, struck out several words and started over. The telegrapher was leaning on the counter. He told the old man two words could be left out entirely which would save the old man money.

In the end the telegrapher rewrote the message, sat down at his key and ignored the watching men across the counter.

This time the telegrapher gestured toward a long bench against the north wall. "I expect they'll answer," he said, and ignored the Cogswells to work at his desk.

The old man tugged out his watch, flipped it open and snapped it closed. He muttered, "They'll be gettin' hungry again."

The rawboned man was not interested. He had pushed out long legs, crossed his arms, tipped down his hat and was asleep.

The telegrapher peered from beneath his eyeshade. "When I was his age I could do that. Go to sleep in the saddle, atop a stage." The telegrapher sighed and went back to work.

Henry Cogswell said he would be at the saloon and left his son sleeping. There were only several old men at a window table playing cards when Cogswell entered. The barman roused himself and nodded.

"What'll it be, Mr Cogswell?"

"Southern Comfort, Pete."

As the barman set up the bottle and glass he said, "This time of year business is usually better."

Cogswell downed his jolt, pushed the glass away and eyed thc saloonman. "You ever think of sellin', Pete?"

The saloonman's eyebrows crawled upwards like caterpillars. "Sell the saloon? You interested in buyin' my saloon?"

"Well, I'm gettin' along. The cattle business is gettin' more complicated, and for a damned fact I'm tired of winter feedin' in snow to my butt an' sweatin' like a stud horse all summer. Now this place is warm in winter, cool in summer an' — "

"Mister Cogswell, you're repeatin'

the story of my life. Freeze in winter, suffer heat stroke in summer. I was in the livestock business for years, grew up in it, and it come to me to save money an' buy into a business where you don't have to buck snow an' . . . "

"It ain't for sale, Pete?"

The barman made a wide sweep of his counter with a moist towel and vigorously shook his head. "No sir, it ain't for sale. Fill your glass, on the house, Mister Cogswell."

The old man tipped his head, swallowed once and was replacing the glass when the telegrapher burst past the door with a yellow paper in one hand. Ignoring the saloonman the telegrapher said, "You got your answer. I couldn't wake your son up so I come myself."

Henry Cogswell took the paper, read it and started for the door. The saloonman wagged his head. He hadn't been paid for the first drink. For a fact the livestock business, even the way Cogswell ran it, which was widely rumoured around town, wore a man out before his time.

The telegrapher was a fast walker, like most sparrow-built folks were. The old man entered the office as the telegraph key began clicking. His son was dead to the world, hadn't moved since the old man had departed.

He went over to roust him, handed the yellow paper over and watched the telegrapher at his clicking key. He was scribbling on paper as the key clicked. The old man shook his head in wonder that anyone could make letters out of that rattling little box.

They left the telegrapher's office and reached the jailhouse before the telegrapher leaned back to re-read what he had taken down. He sat a long time gazing at what he had transcribed. It was a fairly long message and it was addressed to the Sheriff of Bison County, township of Mirage, New Mexico Territory.

At the jailhouse Henry Cogswell read the message aloud. "Money coming by stage. Tell Swindin to move out." It was signed Alonzo Starr.

Sheriff Baron relaxed at his desk. "Four days if he changes coaches often and keeps comin' at night."

"More like three," the greying man said from his slouching position across the room.

Cogswell folded the paper carefully, pocketed it and looked around. "Me'n the sheriff'll stay in town. You lads go on back to the ranch. Chain them bastards real good. We're gettin' to the point that we can't have no slip-ups."

The eldest son wanted to stay in town. His father was adamant. "I rely on you, boy. You take care of things at home. Don't let nothin' go wrong."

As the riders were leaving Terry Cogswell paused to speak quietly to his father. "After this one," he said, "I think I'll leave."

If anyone expected the old man to explode they were disappointed. He simply looked up and nodded. He did not even follow his youngest out with his eyes. After the door closed he said, "Taken after his ma. Always has. Just never had it for hard work. His ma's folks were a mealy bunch."

The sheriff agreed. "For a fact, Henry; he's sendin' someone with the money? What does that mean?"

"It's a sizeable amount, Sheriff. If he sent it by post or by stage, just a satchel of it, you know as well as I do it'd never get here." Cogswell leaned back, the whiskey plus the telegram put him in a mellow mood.

"Sheriff, when're you goin' to retire?"

The dark man might have expected anything but that. He leaned on his desk frowning. "Retire? Never thought about it. Why?"

"We've done right well. When we get the money this time it'll be enough with what else we got, to set back an' watch the world go by."

"Henry, you're not thinkin' of quittin'? We got as slick a business goin' — legal an' all — as anyone ever come up with. Hell, there ain't no end. They'll be drivin' cattle from south to north for longer'n we'll live."

Cogswell stroked his beard. "I expect you're right. You want to visit the saloon?"

Sheriff Baron stood up, looked down and said, "I got to change my shirt. Who dumped water over me?"

"One of my riders, Kent Rogers."

As the dark man went into his storeroom to change shirts he called over his shoulder. "There's somethin' about that feller . . . "

"Why, because he doused you? Come on, I'm dryer'n a sandbox."

The sheriff emerged tucking in his shirt tail. "He didn't have to pour so much water."

Cogswell held the door open as the sheriff got his hat. "A dipper full ain't a lot of water. You want to lock this door?"

"What for? There's no prisoners."

10

A Strange Night

THE ride back to the Cogswell place was made mostly in silence. When they got there and Mort dismounted he collapsed. They carried him to the bunkhouse and got him settled. That crucl-faced bulky man who had ridden with the sheriff waited until they were outside then said, "He should have hit him harder."

Alf bristled and the other man smiled bleakly. "Maybe he's got a busted skull."

Alvarado and the turncoat who had cottoned to him stared steadily until the eldest Cogswell growled for them to sit on the floor while he and his companions got lass ropes from the barn.

The bulky, cruel man remained, leaned on the closed door with a cocked six-gun in his fist. Alf spoke to him. "Semas, what are you stayin' with the sheriff for? He's goin' to get his desserts directly."

The bulky man shrugged beefy shoulders. "Every time I rode out with him he pays better'n any damned cowman."

Alf regarded the large man with obvious contempt but did not speak again.

John Doyle asked when they'd be fed. Alf chimed in. The bulky man answered. "It ain't up to me, it's up to Tom Cogswell. If it was up to me I'd bury the lot of you in a canyon where they'd never find you . . . Alf? They'll bury you'n Mort for changin' sides, I'll bet good money on that."

Cogswell and his companions returned to the bunkhouse each man with coiled lariats on their arms. The man named Semas said, "Why not just hang 'em?"

to the eldest Cogswell, and Terry spoke sharply. "No!"

His brother and several others including Semas gazed steadily at the youngest Cogswell, who was standing near a long table, his back to it, the tie-down over his holstered Colt hanging loose.

John Doyle, Jake Swindin and Carter Alvarado looked at Terry. It dawned on them that his brother and the others were not going to brace the youngest Cogswell. They outnumbered him; they were rough, hard men; the only reason they did not take it up had to be that Terry was deadly fast with a handgun.

His brother tossed ropes on the floor and growled for the prisoners to be tied. John Doyle interrupted by asking again when they would be fed. Semas started to answer as he'd done before when the eldest Cogswell looked at his brother and spoke sullenly. "Feed 'em."

Carter Alvarado took a chance and

asked Terry Cogswell where the deputy federal marshals were, and got a reply as Terry worked at firing up the bunkhouse stove. "They left. I got no idea why or when. Sheriff Baron told my pa the liveryman in town said they'd saddled up and left town."

Terry paused to look at the men sitting on the floor. "I expect you should be tied." He smiled thinly. "I should tell you, at shootin' competitions around no one's ever beat me." The smile widened slightly. "But try me if you want to."

They did not try him, in fact of all their captors he impressed them most favourably.

Carter tried another question. "You fellers got all the Starr cattle on Cogswell range?"

Terry paused to consider Alvarado, did not reply and went to work at the stove.

The short, wiry man named Clark rolled and lighted a smoke. Alf, who knew Clark, Mirage's harnessmaker,

194

inhaled deeply and waited. Clark inhaled and exhaled again, looking squarely at Alf and shook his head.

The day was wearing along and hunger, which was a cumulative affliction, was tormenting the prisoners before Terry began piling food on plates for Clark and the surly large man to put on the table.

Terry looked at the prisoners, told Clark and Semas to eat and joined them without a word or a glance at the prisoners.

Not until those three had finished did Terry jerk his head for the captives to sit at the table.

Because the guards either did not exchange words with the captives or got bored, left and returned to the bunkhouse to ignore the prisoners, time passed uncomfortably.

The sheriff and Henry Cogswell rode out on the second day, conversed on the bunkhouse porch with their friends, looked in briefly at the captives then left taking Jake Swindin with them. Nothing was said about this visit but along toward suppertime the harnessmaker named Clark made a dry comment that each prisoner picked up on. He told Terry Cogswell he had a business in town to take care of, so he'd be glad when the messenger arrived the following day from Alonzo Starr. He also said Jake Swindin was, in his opinion, a lousy drover, and that seemed to satisfy the harnessmaker's increasing irascibility.

Alvarado softly told John Doyle the messenger couldn't possibly arrive from up north the following day. Doyle said nothing.

The morning of the third day while Terry was frying spuds and meat at the cook stove, the bulky mean-eyed man named Semas took the prisoners out to stretch their legs among other things, and slowly came erect, expressionless and troubled.

Alvarado and John Doyle saw the same thing. Five horsemen on a low rim that overlooked the yard, sitting motionless and silent.

Semas herded his prisoners into the bunkhouse, told Terry and Clark to go outside, which they did, and returned considering Semas from slightly narrowed eyes. Clark said, "All right, we went."

Semas's brow furrowed. "You didn't see 'em settin' up there like crows in a tree?"

"See who?"

"Five riders on the rim east of the yard."

Terry went back outside leaving the harnessmaker and Semas arguing. Semas turned to Alvarado and John Doyle. "Tell him what you saw."

Doyle and Alvarado stood like wooden Indians looking steadily at the hulking large man. Neither said a word.

Semas reddened. "You seen 'em, gawddammit."

The pair of captives remained stone-faced and silent.

Semas yanked open the door and nearly collided with young Cogswell as he lunged past the opening. Terry turned slowly to regard the large man from an expressionless face.

The sinewy, shorter man scowled before saying, "Where?"

Semas flung out a rigid large arm. "On that ridge yonder. Five of 'em settin' like stones."

"Lookin' at the yard, was they?"

"Yes. Settin' up there like — "

"Who was it? The sheriff an' Mister Cogswell again?"

"It wasn't neither Cogswell nor the lawman. Gawddammit, I know what I mean. Them damned fellers inside seen 'em too."

Terry spat aside and turned to re-enter the bunkhouse. "You need rest," he dryly said, and left the door open for Semas to use.

The bulky man slapped his hat atop the table glaring at the prisoners. "You seen 'em, gawddammit, don't act dumb. Five riders settin' up yonder like In'ians, except that they wasn't In'ians."

None of the captives responded. In fact they slid their eyes away from the thoroughly upset large man. He started around the table as though to attack the captives. Terry barked at him, "Leave 'em be!"

Semas went to the table, retrieved his hat, slammed it on and left the cabin.

The harnessman and young Cogswell exchanged a look and a shrug. Clark said, "Always acted like he was born with one foot out of the stirrup."

By suppertime Semas had not returned. Clark was indifferent but Terry wasn't and left the cabin to search the yard. By the time the others were through eating Terry returned and this time he was visibly upset.

"His horse is out there but I couldn't find him."

The harnessmaker sucked his teeth in thought, then left the table to also go outside. Before the door closed on him Terry said, "Be careful."

The harnessmaker grunted. He'd

been careful all his life and did not take kindly to some young whippersnapper warning him about being careful.

John Doyle watched Terry Cogswell and eventually said, "Maybe there is someone out there."

"Who?" snapped Terry.

John Doyle replied dryly. "If it ain't your pa or the sheriff, who could it be?"

The elder son of Henry Cogswell whose involvement, up to this time had been cloaked in sullen disagreeableness, arose from the table, hitched at his shell belt and headed for the door as he growled at his brother. "If it ain't Pa nor the sheriff, an' if it ain't some nosy bastard from town, why then I'd say we'd better find 'em."

No one replied. When the door closed behind Terry's brother Orville spoke into the temporary silence. He asked young Cogswell if he believed in haunts, and got such a look of scorn Orville got busy dry-washing his hands.

When dusk arrived Orville Bean went twice to the door and peeked out. Saw nothing and got a cup of lukewarm coffee at the stove. John Doyle sauntered over to also fill a cup. While he was doing this he made a quiet observation. "Ain't no one come back, Mister Cogswell," and paused to briefly sip from the cup. "There is *somethin'* out there an' I'd say it ain't friendly towards us fellers in here."

Terry offered a nervous rebuttal. "My brother can't be snuck up on. He's makin' a big sashay is all."

Doyle took his cup back to his bench and sat down. In a loud whisper he said, "Somethin' that ain't natural is goin' on."

Excepting the scrawny harnessmaker, the guards who had not returned were not individuals to be taken lightly, particularly Terry's brother Tom Cogswell. The bulky man named Semas was unlikely to give ground to a curly bear, but he was not and never had been an individual capable

201

of handling subtlety. He thought with his fists; anyone who did that would eventually meet someone else who thought that way and was bigger or quicker.

Terry worried less about the big, mean man and the harnessmaker than he did about his brother and while they were as different as night was from day, while Terry remained inside sweating, it bothered him that he had always relied on his brother. It had nothing to do with affection, it had everything to do with a subservient individual relying on a dominant individual.

Orville lighted the lamp and hung it from its overhead wire. Terry sat, head cocked in concentration. He did not even look away from the door when Carter Alvarado went to stir coals to life in the stove to make supper.

Terry didn't eat but the others did. Orville glanced from young Cogswell's back to John Doyle, who slowly shook his head. Maybe Orville could have jumped Terry but John Doyle considered it too risky.

They ate in silence, the hanging lamp's mantle hadn't been cleaned in a 'coon's age so the light was wavery and not very bright.

When they finished supper Orville stacked the plates, took them to the large pan of hot greasy water on the stove, dumped them in and once again considered Terry, but this time young Cogswell turned and Orville went to his bench and sat down.

Terry said, "Gawddammit, it ain't like Tom to miss supper."

The captives sat in impassive silence. Orville sucked his teeth until Terry turned fiercely and told him to stop it, which Orville did.

There was a small scratching sound at the door and Terry sprang to his feet, six-gun in hand. The others hadn't seen him draw the gun. He told Orville to open the door. The skinny man arose reluctantly. As he moved ahead he told Terry to be careful with that damned gun.

Every man's attention was fixed on the door as Orville gripped the latch to lift it. Terry cocked his six-gun; in the silence it was a menacingly loud sound. Orville looked at Terry who wigwagged for the door to be opened.

Orville re-gripped the latch, abruptly flung the door inward and jumped against the southerly log wall.

Darkness engulfed the little front porch. No one was standing there. Without a word John Doyle went to the opening, bent and straightened up with his back to the others. Terry snarled at him to get out of the doorway.

John Doyle turned. He was holding a six-gun in his left hand. Terry sucked air. It was his brother's sidearm.

John Doyle kicked the door closed, took the Colt to the table and dropped it. Terry reached, gripped the gun, opened the loading chute and turned the cylinder. The gun was empty. He put the gun atop the table and looked at the men watching him. Orville quietly said, "I told you there was somethin' out there, an' it's not no varmint. No animal snuck up there and left that gun."

Such an obvious observation did not require a response. Terry's face was sweat-shiny in lamplight and it was not very warm in the bunkhouse. He cleared his throat twice, flicked a glance from John Doyle to the gun, and from the gun to Carter Alvarado.

"Open the door an' call out," he told Alvarado.

"Yell what?"

Terry's tongue made a darting circuit of his lips before he answered. "Ask who they are an' what they want."

Carter went to the door but hesitated before opening it. He looked steadily at young Cogswell. "I'll tell you what they want — us who're inside here. They got the scrawny feller, the big dumb ox an' your brother. They want all of us."

"Open the gawdamned door an' talk to 'em," Terry loudly exclaimed.

Alvarado opened the door but stood

on the far side of the opening when he called out. There was no answer so he called again, louder this time.

From the rear of the room someone made a comment. "Whoever they are, if they was here for blood by now there would have been shootin'."

Terry turned on the speaker in a fury, cursed him and said if he opened his mouth one more time he would kill him.

From the wall beside the open door as Carter watched and listened, he wondered if the gentler, more sensitive of the old man's sons was more likely to explode under pressure and maybe kill people, than his larger, more confident and overbearing brother.

Carter leaned and yelled again. This time while there was no verbal reply something sailed past into the lighted room and landed on the floor between the stove and the table.

Orville retrieved it, glanced at his hand and held it out for Terry to take the object.

It was a large, heavy clasp knife with scrimshaw carving on both sides. One side had a carved longhorn cow's head. The opposite side had a large letter C within a circle, the Cogswell brand.

Henry put the knife beside the six-gun and solemnly said, "Tom's castratin' knife," and leaned off the table looking at the impassive, silent prisoners. He wagged his head at Orville. "You ever hear of a haunt that could throw things?" Before the skinny man could respond Terry turned his attention to John Doyle. "If they ain't friends of mine maybe they're friends of yours. You want to talk to 'em?"

Doyle shook his head. "It's clear to me, Mr Cogswell, they don't want to talk, whoever they are."

"You can try," Terry said and John Doyle arose, went to the opposite side of the open door from Carter and called out his name, repeated it twice, and asked for whoever was out there to speak up.

It did not work this time any better

than it had worked the other times. John Doyle kicked the door closed, passed Terry on his way to a bench, sat down and considered the younger Cogswell stonily.

Terry said, "Well . . . ?"

"Set here until daylight," Doyle told him. "Maybe they'll show themselves, but whether they do or not, you're in a bad stew."

Orville spoke up and once again his friends stared. He said, "One of us goes out there. Talks to them fellers. It can't hurt an' it might help."

Terry looked and John Doyle inclined his head. Terry jerked his head for Orville to go to the door as he said, "Let 'em know you're comin' so they don't shoot you."

Orville's reply was cogent. "They ain't used guns yet," and walked out into the night.

The men inside the bunkhouse scarcely breathed as they listened. There was not a sound, no scuffle, no squawk, just silence. Orville returned through the door shrugging his shoulders. "It's too dark to see anythin'. We'll have to wait 'til daylight."

Terry relaxed a little. Alvarado made a guess. "They got this place surrounded."

Terry's forehead creased. "How many are there?"

He got no response. John Doyle went to the stove to refill his coffee mug, as he faced around he said, "Terry, how in hell did you ever get tangled up in this?"

Terry's reply was swift and loud. "He's my pa!"

John Doyle went back to the bench with his cup, sat down and shoved out his legs. "It's their move," he said to no one in particular, "an' I'll tell you one thing, unless that bastard of a lawman shows up come mornin' with plenty of friends, we're goin' to end up captured again."

Outside a horse whinnied, otherwise the night was silent. Time passed, Carter snored and John Doyle kicked his foot. The snoring stopped but Alvarado did not awaken.

Terry picked up the clasp knife. "My pa give him this when he got big enough to rope an' throw a calf."

Terry put the knife aside, got a half-full cup of coffee at the stove, returned to the table, tipped in whiskey and glanced at the prisoners, who looked back. Terry made a tired growl and relaxed. He said, "I'll be damned if I can figure it out but right now it looks like us in here against them out there."

No one offered an explanation, in fact no one spoke.

11

Silhouettes on Horseback

WHEN dawn arrived it was cold despite a peeping sun and would continue to be for several hours. Visibility, for a change, was excellent, and Terry was at the front-wall window scanning the yard and beyond, while the others were clustered at the stove for hot coffee.

They had looked soiled, rumpled and haggard last night by sputtering lamplight; by daylight they looked worse, beard-stubbled, unwashed and haggard.

Terry abruptly said, "I'll be damned. Semas was right. Look out there."

They crowded at the window, captor and captives, some holding coffee mugs.

Orville was noticeably sarcastic when

he said, "Well now, when I was growin' up my granny said it was four horsemen — there's five on that rim. Hold my cup, Terry, I'm goin' out there."

Terry recoiled from accepting the cup so John Doyle took it. He also opened the door, stood in the opening for a long time then eyed the skinny man as he said, "Gawdamned foolishness. No talk, no guns, just settin' up there like strongheart In'ians."

Orville stepped off the meagre little bunkhouse porch walking in the direction of the motionless riders. It was a fair distance but his step never faltered. Inside at the window Carter mused aloud. "I sold that beanpole short."

No one commented, they were still and motionless at the window. They had all sold Orville short.

The sun was climbing. It was in Orville's face so he tipped down his hat. When he was close enough he stopped and showed an empty holster. The five mounted men did not move until he was starting up the low slope then a dark, stocky man with an ivory-stocked Colt swung to the ground, moved to the head of his horse trailing one rein and stood impassively until Orville was closer and made an awkward self-conscious smile. Then the dark, stocky man said, "What's your name?"

"Orville Bean."

"You work for Cogswell?"

"No sir, I ride for Jake Swindin. Young Cogswell's inside watchin' us prisoners. Mister, he's lightnin' fast with a handgun."

The dark man replied dryly. "We know. His brother told us. We want everyone in the bunkhouse to come out unarmed an' line up in the yard." The dark man's tone softened. "You know two of the fellers with me?"

Orville hadn't considered the other four men but now did. "Yes sir. He's a deputy federal lawman. I think his name's Harding or something like that."

"It's Hartley. You know the other one?"

213

"He's the younger federal deputy. Showalter, I think."

The dark, stocky man shifted all his weight to one foot as he spoke again. "That other feller is the US Marshal from Denver. We met on the trail. His name's Phil Barbour. The other feller back a ways is one of my riders. My name is Alonzo Starr. Where's Jake Swindin?"

"Far as I know, Mr Starr, he's in Mirage with Cogswell an' the sheriff."

"Go back down there. Tell 'em all to come out without guns an' line up."

Orville said, "Mr Starr, what happened was — "

"*Go down an' have 'em line up. NOW!*"

The deputy marshal Orville had recognized, barely inclined his head. Orville nodded, faced about and began the hike back.

The watchers at the window waited until Orville was close then went to the table and chairs. When he came in they stared at him but no one spoke.

He talked for a full five minutes, then branched off from facts and told them who the four men were who were with Alonzo Starr.

When he said it seemed Starr thought Jake was in the bunkhouse it became clear that, however he had arrived at the decision, Starr had come to the Cogswell ranch and hadn't gone first to Mirage.

Orville jutted his jaw in Terry Cogswell's direction. "He said no guns." Terry put his handgun on the table after which they all went outside. The sun was showing some warmth as it climbed.

The riders on the ridge sat like statues. Eventually, when it seemed they were satisfied, Alonzo Starr led off. The sun was behind the riders, the lined-up men had to squint.

The dark, stocky man drew rein, dismounted and gazed stonily at the disreputable men facing him. He did not take his eyes off them as he addressed the United States marshal, "See if they got hideouts, Mr Barbour."

The greying man handed his reins to a deputy marshal, approached the line, went over each man, finished in front of Terry Cogswell as he drew forth a blue bandanna and wiped his hands. He said, "What's your name?"

"Terry Cogswell."

The large, greying man shoved the bandanna in a pocket as he spoke again. "I've never run across anyone who waxed the inside of his holster that wasn't a killer."

Terry's eyes did not waver. "A man who rode for us years back taught me that."

Marshal Barbour nodded. "Somebody had to." He faced the dark man. "No hideouts, Mr Starr," and pushed past to enter the bunkhouse. When he reappeared in the doorway he said, "There's a hurt feller in here."

Alf explained. "Friend of mine. Sheriff hit him over the head from behind."

Alonzo Starr asked a question. "Can he ride?"

Alf nodded.

Starr looked from John Doyle to Alvarado. "You fellers with Cogswell?"

Doyle replied dryly. "No. We was tryin' to ambush 'em an' they caught us."

Alonzo Starr spoke curtly. "Take someone, go rig out horses an' ride with us to Mirage." He paused then added a little more in the same brusque tone of voice. "We got three fellers chained in the barn. Leave 'em be. Bring the horses to the tie-rack out front. Go on!"

John Doyle jerked his head for Alvarado to follow him as he headed for the barn. Inside, the harnessmaker, the mean-eyed man and Henry Cogswell's eldest son looked up. They had been chained at the ankles and wrists. They had also been gagged. Cogswell made noises behind his gag. Doyle and Alvarado ignored him, went after horses and rigged them out with

Cogswell snarling and growling.

When they had the horses ready they hoisted the chained men to their feet and took them along to the yard. They had to hop. While the horses were being tied, Alonzo Starr walked over and yanked the gags off. Clark and Semas were quiet but Tom Cogswell turned the air blue with profanity. He and the others had been captured in the dark. They'd been unable to make out much about their captors. Cogswell mistook the tall, greying marshal for the leader of the men who had caught them and cursed him, challenged him to fight if the chains would be removed, right up until Alonzo Starr walked up, slapped Cogswell across the face with his open hand, said his name and stepped back as he told John Doyle to remove Cogswell's chains.

When this had been done the dark man said, "All right, loud mouth how do you want it, fists, knives or guns?"

Cogswell was rubbing his wrists as he studied the man with the ivory-handled six-gun. Terry blurted a warning to his brother

"Leave it be. That's Alonzo Starr."

His brother continued massaging his wrists while he studied the shorter, dark man. Semas growled at Cogswell, "If you won't fight, take my chains off."

The greying federal marshal spoke shortly. "Put 'em on horses, let's go to Mirage. Plenty of time for other things when we get 'em all together."

Chains were removed so the captives could ride astride but their wrists were left chained and as the party left the yard the pair of deputy marshals along with Alvarado, Alf and John Doyle, led horses.

It was warming up. Marshal Barbour and Alonzo Starr rode ahead, occasionally conversing. The cavalcade following them rode facing the sun in silence.

Alf watched Mort, but the reticent man seemed to be much better, although dried blood in his hair and on his shirt made it seem he was worse off. He produced a bottle which had been nearly depleted at the bunkhouse, took an occasional pull on it, shoved it back inside his shirt — and winked at Alf.

Alvarado, riding stirrup with John Doyle, studied the stocky dark man. Starr's spurs were overlaid, engraved silver. His hat was clearly 4 x beaver Stetson. His gun with its ivory grips fitted the hand-carved holster suspended from a carved shell belt with a large sterling buckle, keeper and tip.

Except for those indications of affluence, Alonzo Starr did not look extraordinary. He seemed to be somewhere in his fifties, had black hair and eyes, a slightly beaked nose and a wide slit of a mouth. Carter leaned to speak softly to John Doyle. "He looks like he could chew nails and spit rust."

Without taking his eyes off Alonzo Starr John Doyle replied in the same near whisper, "He's one of the biggest cowmen in Wyoming. He's got holdings up in Montana too. He's got more money'n you'n me'll have if we live to two hunnert — and he's got a reputation for backin' down from nothin' an'll fight a buzz saw."

Carter looked at John Doyle. "You know him?"

"No sir, but I've known who he is for a long time." Doyle put a chilly smile on Alvarado. "They say he's hung more cattle'n horse thieves than you can shake a stick at. Do I know him? Just this well, partner; don't even be in his part of the country if you're figurin' on raidin'."

Carter said, "Does he know you?"

John Doyle hung fire briefly before answering. "No. But if Jake tells him about how him'n me met — "

"Jake wouldn't do that. Hell, except for you we'd have been in more trouble than we was. I know Jake; he don't forget favours."

John Doyle said, "Just in case his memory fails him, I'd take it kindly if you'd refresh it before he talks to Mr Starr."

By mid-afternoon, riding thirsty horses

and with their own parched throats, they had the rooftops of Mirage in sight.

Alonzo Starr dropped back to talk to John Doyle. It was for the most part a cryptic conversation. Doyle lied like a trooper about his meeting with Jake Swindin, how he happened to be in the area and a few other things. Starr may have believed him because he smiled, and anyone who knew the dark man could have attested that short of the Second Coming, Alonzo Starr seemed to find few things in life worth his smiles.

The cavalcade entered Mirage from the north and rode as far as the jailhouse before dismounting. Alonzo Starr was the first to enter. He stood briefly in the doorway then turned toward the federal marshal. "Not here. Circulate around town."

The horses were taken to the livery barn where a surprised and unctuous liveryman helped with the off-saddling. Mister Starr said he wanted the horses put in an empty corral, grained and hayed, and handed the liveryman a small gold coin.

Mort sat on a bench after the off-saddling and continued to sit there as the others departed. When the liveryman approached round-eyed at the dried blood and would have clucked commiseratively Mort fixed him with a steady gaze and said "Where is the sheriff?"

The liveryman had no idea. "He's been busier'n a kitten in a box of shavings the last few days. Last I seen him was with an old rumpled-lookin' cowman out front of the telegraph office. You fellers got business with the law?"

Mort nodded. "We have. With me it's personal. I'm goin' to kill the son of a bitch."

The liveryman remembered some chores he'd neglected and hastened in the direction of the corrals across the alley.

Mort finished the bottle and propped

it on the bench at his side. "Mister Barleycorn," he said, "for a fact you're a real friend."

Mort stood up briefly then sat back down. Everything seemed normal except his legs, they were unsteady; fortunately he was in no hurry. The second time he stood up the legs responded satisfactorily so he struck out for the eatery with no thought of his appearance.

The moment he entered half a dozen diners and the caféman looked at him and froze. Mort sat down at the counter. He ordered a steak, spuds, three cups of black java and pie if there was any.

Several diners departed. Two old gaffers at the far end of the counter where it curved toward the wall, ate, eyed Mort, drank coffee, nudged each other and the one with the fullest beard spoke.

"Mister, you look like you been butcherin' hawgs."

"Fixin' to," Mort replied. "But ain't

found him yet. You gents seen him?"

"Seen who?"

"The sheriff, that miserable son of a bitch."

The old men shook their heads, put silver beside empty plates and departed.

The caféman, a former rangeman with a bad back, chewed a toothpick while eyeing Mort. He refilled the coffee cup, and asked a question. "You feelin' all right?"

"Better'n I felt yestiddy. You don't have a bottle do you?"

The caféman had one in his kitchen but shook his head, set the coffee pot aside and said, "Pardner, you don't need no more. From the looks of you I'd say you already got half a load." After a moment of silently studying Mort he also said, "I don't think you know the sheriff."

Mort's reply was emphatic. "I know him. He hit me over the head from behind."

"Pardner, either wait until you're stone sober or use a shotgun. He's a

225

bad man to cross an' he's good with guns."

Mort finished eating, had a final cup of coffee with the caféman and said, "Folks like him, do they?"

The rangeman-turned-caféman shook his head. "Not any that I know. He's an overbearin' mean, loud-mouthed horse's ass. But he's the law." The caféman spat out his toothpick. "What's your name?"

"Mort."

"Mort what?"

"What difference does that make?"

"All right, Mort. That's what we'll put on your headboard." The caféman brightened a little. "I got a sawed-off scattergun."

Mort arose. "No thanks. What do I owe you?"

"Nothin', a man's last meal is free."

Mort went as far as the doorway before speaking again. "Don't bet no money on him survivin' — pardner."

After Mort had departed the caféman got another toothpick. He had quit chewing six months earlier, toothpicks were a poor substitute; he used about half a box a day.

Several men including the federal marshal and Alonzo Starr were loitering outside the telegraph office. Starr was holding a yellow slip of paper that contained the message the man with the blue eyeshade hadn't sent.

Mort went up there. Alonzo Starr watched him approach and said, "Mr Doyle, take him to the store for a clean shirt."

Doyle dutifully intercepted Mort, steered him in the direction of the emporium and the men with Alonzo Starr stood like storks until the dark man addressed the federal marshal. "You got any questions about what Baron an' Cogswell do with cattle drives through here?"

Phil Barbour shook his head. "But I got to say it's the first time I ever even heard of stealin' cattle within the law."

Starr's dark gaze lingered on the greying man. "Does that bother you?"

Marshal Barbour looked at the pair of deputy marshals when he replied. "No sir, it don't bother me at all." The deputies nodded agreement.

Alonzo Starr ranged a searching gaze southward down the roadway. "Let's split up an' search. He's got to be somewhere around."

The juiceless telegrapher poked his head out the door. "I heard that Swindin feller say he wanted to go look at some cattle he's hired out to drive to Wyoming. He said if some was missin' he wanted a real good excuse. When he delivered up in Wyoming he wanted one hell of a good excuse."

Carter Alvarado put in his two bits' worth. "Cogswell told Jake most of the cattle was on Cogswell's range."

Alonzo Starr was pulling on a pair of doeskin roping gloves when he said, "The livery barn, gents. Fresh horses this time."

They stopped midway to the barn to lock up the Cogswells, Semas, and the harnessmaker.

228

12

The Way Things Happen

A BREEZE came up as the day waned. Visibility at this time of year was excellent until dusk, which would not arrive until close to nine o'clock, so there was no need for haste, which was fortunate because none of the Alonzo Starr riders were familiar with the Cogswell range, but they at least had a partial saving grace, there were fresh shod horse tracks to follow.

It was still a good distance from Mirage. At least their horses were fresh. They talked on the way; Starr was able to fill in the blank spots concerning his missing cattle, how the rustling had been accomplished until, by the hour they had buildings in sight he was impressed. He did not say so, but he was alone in bleak admiration for how his cattle had been taken.

In fact he told John Doyle and Carter Alvarado that he'd caught his share of livestock thieves — without saying what disposal he'd made of them — but this was the first time he'd ever even heard of how livestock could be legitimately stolen.

John Doyle agreed without mentioning that it had been at his instigation that the cattle had been scattered although it might not have made much difference to the dark, dominating individual riding stirrup with him. Alonzo Starr wanted his cattle, as a direct, uncomplicated individual that and little else mattered — except hanging the sons of bitches who had tried to hold him up to recover them.

It was John Doyle who saw the first herd about a hundred or so head grazing over a mile area. Starr proved his savvy by riding a mile northward before turning southward in the direction of the cattle.

They might have stampeded at sight of horses approaching, but several cows with baby calves squared around and pawed. The other critters did not flee but remained poised to.

Alonzo Starr veered westerly, led the ride down that side of the cattle, halted when he had seen all that was necessary, mopped his forehead and shot John a dark look. "Mine, every damned last one of 'em. Doyle, they aren't too fleshy."

Doyle had the answer to that. "Drove cattle hardly ever put on weight while they're movin'."

Mister Starr stood in his stirrups briefly then sank down. He had seen cattle but no horsemen. He wondered aloud if maybe Cogswell and Swindin hadn't made their sashay hours earlier and might now be at the yard.

No one suggested anything different so the dark cowman swung back to retrace their way until they had the buildings in sight.

Starr halted, hands atop the horn.

There were no animals tied to any of the hitching poles. When he mentioned this Carter said, "Most likely stalled in the barn," and Alonzo Starr nodded. "Go have a look, on foot, we'll stay out of sight until you get back."

Carter swung down, handed up his reins, leaned to remove both spurs, buckle them together and looped them around the saddle horn.

Mister Starr watched and as Carter was moving away asked why he'd left his spurs behind, and got a one syllable reply. "Dog."

Starr waited until Carter was on the west side of the barn before dismounting and leading the way back a short distance. At this new position he asked John Doyle if he knew Carter Alvarado, and Doyle could only reply based on their short acquaintanceship, but John Doyle was a good reader of men so he used a little salsa when he replied.

"Well enough. He's a top hand, takes orders good, works hard an' don't

232

drink — well — not much anyway. Good with livestock."

Starr said no more. He leaned on his horse watching the buildings. Eventually he said, "Well, there's a trickle of smoke. Somebody's down there. Does Cogswell have a wife?"

No one answered because no one knew of a certainty if he did or not until John Doyle said, "I don't think so."

Starr spat and reset his hat, although the lowering sun was at his back. "Boys, let me tell you somethin'. I'm a sight older'n any of you an' I've learned a few things. A man's no good in direct proportion to the length of time he don't have a good woman."

They regarded the dark, stocky man stoically. None of them had ever heard that before; in fact most of them had never known a good woman. John Doyle risked a personal question, which was the epitome of bad manners among frontiersmen. "You married, Mr Starr?"

Ordinarily Alonzo Starr might have glared in silence. Right now he had other things on his mind so he answered. "Fourteen years, Mr Doyle. Finest woman I ever knew. Her name's Eagle Woman."

That settled the minds of his companions about one thing. Alonzo Starr was an Indian.

Carter returned with a reddening sun in his face. "Three horses in the barn."

Starr and John Doyle stared. "Three?"

Alvarado'd had time to ponder this so he offered two opinions. "Either the telegrapher was wrong, or maybe they picked up another rider out here."

Alonzo Starr hunkered in long silence. For some reason he had never tried to understand, the idea of fighting after sundown made him uncomfortable. He looked over his shoulder, the reddening sun was a small distance from going down behind some distant sawtooth ridges. He stood up, made sure the cinch was tight and without a word swung astride. He led off in the same direction Carter had used; the barn blocked the view from the house.

As they swung off out back there was the sound of a door slamming. John Doyle reacted by flinging up an arm to keep the horses and men out of sight along the rear barn wall, and as they were doing this John Doyle peeked inside the barn, sprang around the opening with a Colt in his fist and flattened in the gloom without moving.

The man who entered the barn was humming. He plucked a three-tined hay fork from its wall pegs and started for the loft ladder when John Doyle spoke softly from shadows.

"Right where you are, mister!"

The humming stopped, the man froze with a fork in his right hand, his left hand on a rung of the ladder.

John Doyle said, "Walk toward the back door with that fork in both your hands."

The startled man did exactly as he'd been told. The moment he cleared the door a powerful pair of hands grabbed him. He would have fallen if he hadn't dropped the hay fork. The dark man lifted him straight and slammed him against the logs at his back. The man was a stranger to his captors. The face of the dark man was no farther than eight inches away, and the black eyes were murderous.

Carter emptied the man's holster. As this was being done the frightened captive blurted out a protest. "What the hell . . . what you fellers want? Who are you?"

Starr pulled the man forward and slammed him back against the logs. "Who's in the house?"

"Mister Cogswell, a man name of Jake Swindin, an' the sheriff."

"Who are you?"

"I ride for Cogswell. Name's Nat Hawthorne."

"Do you? Where the hell you been the last few days?"

"At a line camp, sixteen miles north-west of here."

"You got cattle up there?"

"Yes, quite a bunch. Henry and his oldest boy drove 'em up last week."

Carter Alvarado stepped up, pushed Alonzo Starr's arms away, and as the frightened cowboy relaxed Carter asked how long he'd worked for Henry Cogswell. The answer was spoken in a more relaxed voice. "Off'n on two, three years. My folks got a stump ranch back in the hills. It's closer to the line camp than Cogswell's yard, so when he buys a big herd he drives 'em up yonder an' hires me to mind 'em."

Carter faced Alonzo Starr. "That's where the rest of your cattle'll be."

Starr nodded still glaring at Nat Hawthorne. "What's the mark on them cattle?" he growled and again Alvarado interrupted. "They're yours, we know that. Right now I'd like to see the inside of the house." Carter faced the cowboy again. "You come down to toss feed, did you?"

"Yes."

"How long before they'll miss you?"

Hawthorne shrugged. "I don't know. Fifteen minutes. Maybe more."

Carter pointed. "Sit down, legs together arms behind your back."

Hawthorne sat but as they leaned to chain him he said, "Who are you fellers? Is Mr Cogswell in trouble? I been hirin' on with him for some time, an' he pays on time. One of his boys comes up now'n then, a sort of quiet feller."

They gagged Nat Hawthorne, made certain he had no other weapons, propped him against a stall door and went out back to palaver.

Alonzo Starr let Carter speak first, and while Alvarado was doing this the dark man watched him. When the discussion was finished he asked Carter a blunt question. "You part In'ian?"

Carter's stare showed annoyance at the personal question but he answered it. "Half Mex. My mother was a homesteader's daughter."

Carter's obvious hostility made Alonzo Starr show one of his rare smiles. He jerked his head. "Lead off. It ain't full dark yet. Be careful."

Alvarado's resentment had not cooled. "Maybe you'd better lead off — tomahawk."

John Doyle's breath stopped for three seconds. Alonzo Starr faced forward slowly, looked steadily at Carter, then laughed. They had never heard him laugh before.

He faced southward, Carter's hostility was diminishing as he and John Doyle followed the stocky, dark man.

There were outbuildings, a bunkhouse, a well house and a smoke house on the west side of the yard. They provided shelter for the stalkers but not well as would have been the case elsewhere, across the yard was a shoeing shed, a large storehouse of some kind and a three-sided wagon and buggy shed.

They would have had more protection if they'd been on the east side but they dared not walk over there now, and with failing daylight they could stalk the main house well enough from the west side.

As they moved away from the barn a horse whinnied. They froze but no one emerged from the house. They got behind the well house and paused. The aroma of cooking was clear even at that distance because the little breeze was still blowing.

They were preparing to make the final crossing to the west side of the house when a screaming man burst from the barn yelling all the way to the porch. They caught glimpses of him from behind buildings. It was Nat Hawthone. At the moment no one understood how he had somehow freed himself, that would come later, nor, actually would it matter. What did matter was that moments after he reached the house the lamps went out.

Carter said, "Forted up. Now what?"

Alonzo Starr pushed away from shelter, there remained sufficient visibility to show movement, if not clearly what was making it.

Someone fired from the house. The muzzleblast was no more than a pinprick of light. Alonzo Starr fired back so quickly John Doyle and Alvarado wondered whether the gunman would have had time to leap aside.

Evidently he'd had the time because the next gunfire from the house came from two handguns. This time Alonzo Starr got back to shelter. One sleeve was torn but there was no bleeding. He spoke matter-of-factly to the men behind him. "One of 'em's a good shot."

Carter made an unnecessary comment. "What'd you expect, steppin' out in plain sight?"

Alonzo Starr neither replied nor looked around. His full attention was on the house. When he finally spoke he said, "Fire it. There's coal oil somewhere around, soak some rags an' burn 'em out."

Neither Carter nor John Doyle

seemed inclined to try this. Alonzo Starr turned on them. "It'll be dark soon. Find the coal oil!"

Carter did not move but John Doyle did, he went back in the direction of the barn, was gone a long time before returning to say he'd had no luck.

Alonzo Starr studied the opposite buildings, mumbled something about the shoeing shed, then in a clearer voice he said, "I'll run for it, you boys keep firin' until I'm over there."

He ran, a sprinting phantom in the failing light. The men he'd left behind fired at windows, at the front door, and kept it up. They must have been successful because no one fired back and the dark man disappeared among the opposite buildings. As the men were reloading Alvarado said, "Damned fool. We'd do better to wait until it's plumb dark."

John Doyle did not comment. When his handgun was freshly charged he eased around the wall of the shelter. The yard was deathly silent. Carter remembered a dog; evidently gunfire had driven it quaking under the house. Whatever had happened to it there was no barking, nor even a sighting.

The first inkling the men behind the shelter had that Starr had been successful was not opposite, in the direction of the shoeing shed, but on the east side of the house where flames abruptly brightened the night from that direction.

In awe John Doyle said, "I'll be damned."

About the time Carter got up where he could see, the flames seemed to be taking hold. The main house was old, its logs had been sucked dry of moisture over many years. They did not burn well at first, but they burned and someone, probably Nat Hawthorne who was evidently given to screaming, yelled "Fire! Fire!"

As the flames became brighter a winded Alonzo Starr returned to the west side shelter. Carter and John Doyle could see his grinning, dark face reflected by firelight. He looked to them something from *tierra inferno*, but that impression lasted only moments, yelling men inside the house were finally aware of what had happened.

Alonzo Starr looked over his shoulder where the day was finally dying, made an overhead motion with one arm and ran. As long as there was shelter John Doyle and Carter followed, but when there was no more shelter they paused. Alonzo Starr did not slacken his pace, he was heading for the porch in a straight line.

Carter threw out an arm but the gesture was unnecessary, John Doyle hadn't come down in the last rain. He had no intention of being as foolhardy as the Wyoming rancher.

They watched and waited. Alonzo Starr hit the door with all his weight. It groaned but did not yield. He lowered his handgun and fired at the hasp, bits of steel flew in all directions. Moments later Alonzo Starr disappeared inside. Carter said it again. "Damned fool," and this time John Doyle agreed, but silently. He was holding his breath.

There was a single gunshot inside the house then three more in rapid succession, and after the last shout a high yell.

John Doyle loosened a little. "I've heard that yell before. If he can do that he's still standin' up, but I wouldn't bet a copper he will be for long."

Carter again said it, "Damned fool."

The entire east side of the house was burning. The tongues of orange flame found the cedar shake roof, as dry as tinder, and began licking along it.

A man taller and more rawboned than Alonzo Starr was highlighted by flame as he appeared in the doorway. Carter said, "Jake."

John Doyle added a little more. "He don't look good."

Behind Jake Swindin the shorter, stockier man appeared, six-gun in a firm grip. With that reddening sun only half size in the sooty sky, Alonzo Starr prodded Jake Swindin in the direction of the barn. The older man walked like a dog passing a peach seed, with justification; he had been tied hard and left lying shortly before the fight started.

When he saw John Doyle and Carter his stride lengthened slightly. Alonzo Starr did not leather his ivory-stock six-gun until they were all in the barn, then he turned to watch the house burn. He had blood showing in the inside of his right leg. Firelight showed more, his face had the same wild look his companions from the barn had seen before. When he faced around, Jake was sitting on a horseshoe keg. Alvarado and John Doyle were standing close by.

After one more look in the direction of the fiercely burning house Alonzo Starr walked over, yanked Jake off the keg and sat down ignoring the others until he had used a bandanna to tie off the bleeding, then he looked up and addressed them. "That's how you take care of sons of bitches like that.

If you can't hang 'em."

Carter had a question. "The cowboy too?"

Starr worked on his wound as he replied. "No! He must have left out the back door. But the other two, Cogswell and the lawman — yes. I give 'em a chance, an' they turned but they was too scairt of the fire to shoot straight."

He looked for the federal officers, who had managed to avoid the fighting. When he stared back he shook his head. "Self-defence, two against one. No witnesses."

Alonzo Starr stood up. "We'll commence a roundup tomorrow. Right now let's get back to Mirage. I'm hungry an' thirsty."

Carter and John Doyle exchanged looks, took the marshal with them, and out back Carter said, "He acted crazy."

Marshal Barbour spoke quietly. "They don't fight at night. He wanted it over with before it got dark."

Carter stopped what he was doing, so did John Doyle. "He liked to have got himself killed for somethin' like that?" Alvarado asked, and the tall federal officer inclined his head without any further elaboration.

When they led the animals inside Jake and Alonzo Starr were talking. Of the two Jake looked worse off than the man with the bloody pants leg. As soon as the horses appeared the conversation terminated.

There was heat the full width and breadth of the house as they left the yard. Carter caught a flashing glimpse of a dog running as swiftly as it could.

Before they reached Mirage Alonzo Starr rode with the federal marshal. When their discussion terminated Marshal Barbour veered off in the direction of the northerly roadway. It was a hell of a long distance to Denver.

Fire on a moonless night was visible for one hell of a distance. As the men with Alonzo Starr rode down the main roadway in the direction of the livery barn, word was already spreading.

The soiled, haggard horsemen had gone in the direction of the Cogswell place and they had now returned leaving a fiercely burning fire in the dark distance.

Alonzo Starr left them at the livery barn to go in search of help for his wounded leg. He had ridden most of the way to Mirage with gritted teeth. The graze was on the inside of the leg, the side which rubbed the saddle fender.

Jake led off in the direction of the saloon where their haggard, disreputable appearance brought silence. The barman eyed them from an expressionless face. Only one man broke the silence, a tawny-eyed cowman who sounded sarcastic when he said, "Took care of ol' Cogswell, did you?"

Carter looked around from the bar. "And the sheriff too."

Response encouraged the stockman.

"Gunfight, was it?"

Garter fixed the cowman with a steady gaze. "Ride out and see for yourself," he said, downed his jolt and followed the others down to the café.

Before they entered Jake asked about the lawmen. John Doyle told him. "I heard the big feller from Denver tell the other two to go on back where they come from." At Jake's soft frown John Doyle shrugged. "They'd have reason, I expect. It wouldn't look right them buyin' into a private fight, would it?"

The caféman's toothpick stopped moving when the weary, worn-down men walked in. As they eased down at the counter he said, "Where's Mort?"

They looked up blankly.

"He's somewhere around. He's goin' to kill the sheriff."

Carter said, "Steak, if you got it, spuds an' coffee."

The caféman went to his kitchen.

John Doyle said, "Where'n hell is Mort?"

No one answered, the caféman

250

brought hot coffee and the topic of the quiet man evaporated with the fumes.

They ate in dogged silence. Other diners appeared, mostly more curious than hungry, and about the time they were finished several riders who had switched sides appeared but asked no question of the men who had left them behind to ride to the Cogswell place.

When they were finished they crossed to the jailhouse, brought the pair of Cogswells to the office and solemnly told them what had happened — the old man and Sheriff Baron had perished in the fire.

Terry, the younger Cogswell, sat down, his truculent brother remained standing. He seemed on the verge of denunciation. Terry spoke to him quietly. "I told you'n Pa it would end somethin' like this. Tom, leave it be. It's too late to change anythin'. Set down."

They waited until the rawboned elder son sat, then John Doyle told them they could go. He said that although the house was no longer standing Cogswell land was extensive enough to start over. Terry nodded in a dull-eyed way. His brother neither nodded nor spoke.

Carter went outside for a smoke. John Doyle joined him out there. He asked if Alvarado would like to work for Alonzo Starr and got a sly small smile as Carter answered, "Maybe. Someday."

"He'll hire you on."

"Yeah; well — you remember that cow outfit with the woman'n girl alone? The place we stopped at for fresh horses when we come out of the — "

Doyle answered impatiently. "I remember, the woman had a face like a meat axe. What about 'em?"

"You remember that girl's name?"

John Doyle's frown was slow coming. "I never heard her name."

"Yes you did. Her ma called her Tami."

"What about her?"

"I'm goin' back there."

John Doyle's frown deepened. "That woman'll skin you alive. I seen how she watched that girl."

Carter arose, yawned and stretched, glanced in the direction of the livery barn, and its loft of fragrant hay as he said, "They run cattle an' I work cheap." He smiled at John Doyle. "Tell Mr Starr if things don't work out I'll come see him up in Wyoming."

They shook hands. The last John Doyle ever saw of Carter Alvarado was his night-shadowed silhouette walking in the direction of the livery barn.

The following noon Alonzo Starr appeared at the café, limping but otherwise looking no different. He stood to be fed, paid for breakfast and outside when he asked about Alvarado, John Doyle told him. Starr's dark eyes brightened slightly as he changed the subject. "Swindin, maybe we can hire hands to round up the cattle and get the drive goin' north again."

Jake nodded. "It'll likely take time, Mr Starr."

"I expect it will. I'll send riders south to meet you. Now, I bought passage on the northbound stage." Starr extended his hand, said no more and limped across the road in the direction of the corral yard.

As John Doyle watched the departing cowman he asked Jake if Starr had said anything about him. Jake shook his head. "Not a lot an' I didn't say much either. Mr Doyle, I'd like to hire you an' your friends to help with the roundup an' the drive north."

John Doyle smiled at the older man. "All right. It'll be the first time in years since I drove cattle for other folks."

They shook hands.

The scrawny telegrapher wearing his blue eyeshade came down where they were standing. "Is it true the sheriff and old Cogswell is dead?"

Jake nodded.

The telegrapher stiffened. "Gents, I expect I knew as much as anyone about their cattle ransomin' business, an' I got to tell you I knew that someday the good Lord's retribution would catch up with 'em."

After the telegrapher had hiked back to his office John Doyle said, "I think it was more Samuel Colt than Gawd that caught up with 'em. You like to visit the saloon with me, before we start roundin' up cattle?"

For the second time when they entered the saloon there was silence. as they leaned on the bar Jake Swindin said, "Samuel Colt? The law of retribution? I didn't know Gawd was an In'ian."

THE END

FIGHTING RAMROD
Charles N. Heckelmann

Most men would have cut their losses, but Frazer counted the bullets in his guns and said he'd soak the range in blood before he'd give up another inch of what was his.

LONE GUN
Eric Allen

Smoke Blackbird had been away too long. The Lequires had seized the Blackbird farm, forcing the Indians and settlers off, and no one seemed willing to fight! He had to fight alone.

THE THIRD RIDER
Barry Cord

Mel Rawlins wasn't going to let anything stand in his way. His father was murdered, his two brothers gone. Now Mel rode for vengeance.

ARIZONA DRIFTERS
W. C. Tuttle

When drifting Dutton and Lonnie Steelman decide to become partners they find that they have a common enemy in the formidable Thurston brothers.

TOMBSTONE
Matt Braun

Wells Fargo paid Luke Starbuck to outgun the silver-thieving stagecoach gang at Tombstone. Before long Luke can see the only thing bearing fruit in this eldorado will be the gallows tree.

HIGH BORDER RIDERS
Lee Floren

Buckshot McKee and Tortilla Joe cut the trail of a border tough who was running Mexican beef into Texas. They stopped the smuggler in his tracks.

BRETT RANDALL, GAMBLER
E. B. Mann

Larry Day had the choice of running away from the law or of assuming a dead man's place. No matter what he decided he was bound to end up dead.

THE GUNSHARP
William R. Cox

The Eggerleys weren't very smart. They trained their sights on Will Carney and Arizona's biggest blood bath began.

THE DEPUTY OF SAN RIANO
Lawrence A. Keating and
Al. P. Nelson

When a man fell dead from his horse, Ed Grant was spotted riding away from the scene. The deputy sheriff rode out after him and came up against everything from gunfire to dynamite.

FARGO: MASSACRE RIVER
John Benteen

The ambushers up ahead had now blocked the road. Fargo's convoy was a jumble, a perfect target for the insurgents' weapons!

SUNDANCE: DEATH IN THE LAVA
John Benteen

The Modoc's captured the wagon train and its cargo of gold. But now the halfbreed they called Sundance was going after it . . .

HARSH RECKONING
Phil Ketchum

Five years of keeping himself alive in a brutal prison had made Brand tough and careless about who he gunned down . . .

FARGO: PANAMA GOLD
John Benteen

With foreign money behind him, Buckner was going to destroy the Panama Canal before it could be completed. Fargo's job was to stop Buckner.

FARGO:
THE SHARPSHOOTERS
John Benteen

The Canfield clan, thirty strong were raising hell in Texas. Fargo was tough enough to hold his own against the whole clan.

PISTOL LAW
Paul Evan Lehman

Lance Jones came back to Mustang for just one thing — revenge! Revenge on the people who had him thrown in jail.

HELL RIDERS
Steve Mensing

Wade Walker's kid brother, Duane, was locked up in the Silver City jail facing a rope at dawn. Wade was a ruthless outlaw, but he was smart, and he had vowed to have his brother out of jail before morning!

DESERT OF THE DAMNED
Nelson Nye

The law was after him for the murder of a marshal — a murder he didn't commit. Breen was after him for revenge — and Breen wouldn't stop at anything . . . blackmail, a frameup . . . or murder.

DAY OF THE COMANCHEROS
Steven C. Lawrence

Their very name struck terror into men's hearts — the Comancheros, a savage army of cutthroats who swept across Texas, leaving behind a bloodstained trail of robbery and murder.

SUNDANCE: SILENT ENEMY
John Benteen

A lone crazed Cheyenne was on a personal war path. They needed to pit one man against one crazed Indian. That man was Sundance.

LASSITER
Jack Slade

Lassiter wasn't the kind of man to listen to reason. Cross him once and he'll hold a grudge for years to come — if he let you live that long.

LAST STAGE TO GOMORRAH
Barry Cord

Jeff Carter, tough ex-riverboat gambler, now had himself a horse ranch that kept him free from gunfights and card games. Until Sturvesant of Wells Fargo showed up.

McALLISTER ON THE COMANCHE CROSSING
Matt Chisholm

The Comanche, McAllister owes them a life — and the trail is soaked with the blood of the men who had tried to outrun them before.

QUICK-TRIGGER COUNTRY
Clem Colt

Turkey Red hooked up with Curly Bill Graham's outlaw crew. But wholesale murder was out of Turk's line, so when range war flared he bucked the whole border gang alone . . .

CAMPAIGNING
Jim Miller

Ambushed on the Santa Fe trail, Sean Callahan is saved by two Indian strangers. But there'll be more lead and arrows flying before the band join Kit Carson against the Comanches.

GUNSLINGER'S RANGE
Jackson Cole

Three escaped convicts are out for revenge. They won't rest until they put a bullet through the head of the dirty snake who locked them behind bars.

RUSTLER'S TRAIL
Lee Floren

Jim Carlin knew he would have to stand up and fight because he had staked his claim right in the middle of Big Ike Outland's best grass.

THE TRUTH ABOUT SNAKE RIDGE
Marshall Grover

The troubleshooters came to San Cristobal to help the needy. For Larry and Stretch the turmoil began with a brawl and then an ambush.

WOLF DOG RANGE
Lee Floren

Will Ardery would stop at nothing, unless something stopped him first — like a bullet from Pete Manly's gun.

DEVIL'S DINERO
Marshall Grover

Plagued by remorse, a rich old reprobate hired the Texas Troubleshooters to deliver a fortune in greenbacks to each of his victims.

GUNS OF FURY
Ernest Haycox

Dane Starr, alias Dan Smith, wanted to close the door on his past and hang up his guns, but people wouldn't let him.